"A beautifully written story of life and hope, one that will touch your heart long after you turn the last page."

—SHERRY KYLE,
author of *The Heart Stone* and *Delivered with Love*

"I highly recommend this powerful story and hope its narrative helps motivate this generation to shape a culture of life."

—DANIEL DARLING,
pastor and author of *Teen People of the Bible* and *iFaith*

"Beautifully rich and heartwarming characters. . . . Kathi deftly tackles the topic of an unplanned pregnancy with wisdom and warmth, gentleness, and a healing touch of God's love."

—SUSAN MATHIS,
coauthor of *The Remarriage Adventure*
and *Countdown for Couples*

"In *The Doctor's Christmas Quilt*, Kathi Macias has beautifully woven the story of three women, one from history, two from today, into a tapestry of what it takes to make one's dreams come true despite the obstacles put into one's path."

—MARTHA ROGERS,
author of *Love Stays True*,
Book 1 of "The Homeward Journey" series

Other Fiction Titles
by Kathi Macias

"QUILT" series

The Moses Quilt

"FREEDOM" series

Deliver Me from Evil
Special Delivery
The Deliverer

CHRISTMAS books

A Christmas Journey Home: Miracle in the Manger
Unexpected Christmas Hero

The DOCTOR'S CHRISTMAS QUILT

WILL THIS GIFT GIVE HER *the* COURAGE *to* STAND BY HER CONVICTIONS?

KATHI
MACIAS

NEW HOPE
PUBLISHERS
Gospel-Centered. Missions-Driven.

BIRMINGHAM, ALABAMA

New Hope® Publishers
P. O. Box 12065
Birmingham, AL 35202-2065
NewHopeDigital.com
New Hope Publishers is a division of WMU®.

Library of Congress Control Number: 2013942348

Cover Design: Left Coast Design

ISBN-10: 1-59669-388-6
ISBN-13: 978-1-59669-388-3

N134129 • 0913 • 3M1

Dedicated to the millions of preborn babies who didn't live to take their first breath, but who are now held safely in the Father's arms, and to all those who valiantly take a stand in their defense.

Dedicated also to my beloved husband and children, and to my Lord who has blessed me with such a wonderful family.

Prologue

Dr. Laura Branson clicked out of the Skype conversation and sighed. It had been a positive exchange, and it seemed the half dozen young women had responded well to her pro-life presentation. Still, for every female medical student she influenced, Laura knew there were a dozen others staunchly entrenched in the pro-choice mind-set. And that meant more and more preborn babies would die every year.

She rose from the chair in front of her desk and exited her bedroom, which often served as her "office away from the office." She'd been sitting long enough and needed to move around a bit. Besides, a cold drink might perk her up and enable her to complete the rest of the work she had set aside for the day.

This is supposed to be your day off, she scolded herself silently as she opened the door to the nearly empty fridge and peered inside. *When are you actually going to take a real day off and stop being such a workaholic? Isn't that something you regularly caution medical students and even your colleagues about?*

Laura pulled out a chilled bottle of no-calorie, no-carb, citrus-flavored iced tea and twisted the lid. Hot tea might be more appropriate for the weather on this mid-November Thursday afternoon, but her modest one-story Colorado

Springs home was warm and cozy—so much so that she needed a wake-up jolt more than a warm drink.

The thought of the enthusiastic young women she'd just met via her computer teased her thoughts. *Enthusiastic and young. That describes them to a T. Unlike me, who has long since passed up young and whose enthusiasm needs all the help it can get these days.*

She took a swig of iced tea and wandered back to her room, mentally contrasting the youthful appearance of the medical students on the other end of her Skype conversation with the image of herself that had been so prominently displayed on the students' computers throughout the session. Because she was working at home today rather than at the clinic, she hadn't bothered with makeup and had scarcely run a comb through her short, wavy locks. Though she'd tried to ignore her face on the computer screen, she had noticed more than once that it was time to touch up her roots again. She knew it was vain, but her red-gold hair had been her pride and joy her entire life, and she wasn't ready to trade it in for silver streaks quite yet.

After all, it's not like I'm a senior citizen. Forty-eight is still young . . . or so they say. She smirked. *Whoever "they" may be. People long past forty-eight, no doubt. All I know is, I'm looking fifty in the eyeball, and I still feel like I have so much work I want to do before I leave this planet and move on to my permanent home. Am I being silly, Lord? Should I just take an early retirement and leave medicine to the younger generation? After all, Megan's following in my footsteps. Who better to pass the torch to? Is it time?*

The silent *not yet* resounded in her heart, and she smiled, settling back down in her chair and laying her hand on top of her wireless mouse. So, she might have gray roots and her enthusiasm and energy tended to lag on occasion, but apparently God wasn't through with her yet. And that was just the encouragement she needed to press ahead with her day's plans.

Chapter 1

MEGAN FELT INSULATED from the cold and gray outside her car as she barreled south on I-25 toward the Springs, thankful for the lack of ice on the road but wondering if she'd ever break through the chill that gripped her heart.

"What am I going to tell her, Lord?" she whispered. "*How* am I going to tell her? This is going to break her heart." Her own heart constricted at the greatest question echoing in her mind: *How much* would she tell her?

The thought of her mother, so strong in her convictions and successful in her career, washed over her yet again, as it had so many times in the past few days. She had vacillated between behaving like an adult and keeping the news to herself, at least until the Christmas holidays, and giving in to her childishness by racing home to pour out her heart and let her mama kiss her boo-boo. Obviously the latter had won out, as she was now less than fifteen minutes from home.

Mom will probably be there today. When I talked to her a couple of days ago, she said this was her day off—which means she's working at home, rather than at the clinic. Mom is so disciplined, and such a workaholic. I just wish I had half of her dedication. Maybe if I did I wouldn't be in this mess right now.

A gust of wind rocked her tiny three-year-old hybrid car, reminding her of how much Alex had always despised the vehicle.

"A wannabe car," he'd said the moment he first laid eyes on it. "Dangerous. They should be banned. You're not getting me in that death trap. I don't care how environmentally friendly they're supposed to be. They're definitely not accident friendly."

True to his word, Alex had never ridden in her little car, regardless of how many arguments she offered him about its great gas mileage. Instead they had spent every outing during their six-month relationship riding around in his five-year-old SUV, which Megan complained required a ladder to get inside.

She could hear his laugh now, and the very memory nearly suffocated her with pain. "Maybe if you weren't so short, it wouldn't be a problem," he'd teased her the first time she'd referred to the vehicle's height. Then he'd gently taken her arm and helped her up, reassuring her that he really liked the fact that she was petite, despite his comment. Megan could have climbed into the truck herself, of course, but at the time she took advantage of his offer as an excuse to feel his strength and closeness.

What had she been thinking? How foolish had she been to believe she loved Alex, or even knew him, after only six months? She should have run while she had the chance. But it was too late now. He'd shown his true colors, and she was done with him.

She blinked back the hint of tears, all too familiar these past few weeks, and pushed on. Though she had no idea how she would broach the subject with her mother once she got home, at least she knew she'd be in familiar territory. And despite the fact that her mom would no doubt be crushed at the news, Megan also knew she would receive the much needed support and encouragement that she longed for— though she would have to be careful to keep her story within safe boundaries.

That's the kind of mom you are, Megan thought, pushing back the guilt that nagged at her. *Supportive. Understanding.*

And not just to me. To everyone! Why else would you spend your medical career working at a clinic for the poor rather than in private practice where the money is? It's the reason we stayed in our cookie-cutter track home all these years instead of moving to something bigger and fancier, something in one of the neighborhoods where most other doctors live.

She smiled at the fresh reminder of her mother's altruism and wondered if she'd ever be able to truly follow in Dr. Laura Branson's footsteps—especially now. The familiar, nagging question of whether she was going to medical school solely to please her mother or because it's what she truly wanted crossed her mind, but she shoved it back down.

"I'm sorry, Mama," she whispered, feeling as if she were rehearsing for the speech she would deliver in the next couple of days. "Truly I am. I know how much you sacrificed to put me through medical school, especially with the modest income you make from the clinic. If it wasn't for Dad's insurance money, we'd never have made it. I just hope I haven't crushed your dreams for my future. It's not that I'm giving up on them, but . . . but first I need to tell you my news, even though I know it's probably the last thing you want to hear."

The dark memory of her last date with Alex sent a jagged slice of pain through her heart. This time the tears nearly won out, but she blinked again and kept driving.

"What was I thinking?" she said aloud. "I mean, it's not like I'm some impressionable young teen who doesn't know better? I'm twenty-one years old, for heaven's sake! What is wrong with me? Why did I ever trust him? And why was I so stupid to let myself get into that situation?" She shook her head, trying to stave off the shame that always accompanied these all too familiar thoughts.

"The worst part was that you thought we could go on after that . . . that night." She swallowed, suppressing a shiver at the memory of the large brown eyes that had once melted her heart. "I never want to see your face again, Alex Williams, or hear your voice, or—"

Stop it! she told herself. *You can't afford to start crying while you're driving. Keep your eyes and mind on the road! Besides, it's not like he's pining over you. From the moment he realized you were serious about not wanting to see him anymore, he moved right on to his next victim.*

Despite her anger and loathing toward the man she once thought she loved, she was shocked at how quickly he started strutting around campus with his new girlfriend on his arm. The first time she'd seem them together, she'd found herself gasping for air, like a fish plucked from the water and thrown onto the cold, hard ground. She told herself she was well rid of him, but her insides clenched in rebellion at the thought.

It was only the second time in Megan's almost twenty-two years of life that her heart had been broken. The first time was when her father and younger brother had been killed in a car crash—driving on this same interstate during a blizzard—leaving her and her mother to carry on alone. Losing half her family in one brutal blow had left the then twelve-year-old girl reeling.

All the more reason Mom and I grew closer than ever. And she's going to understand what's happened, what I'm going through now—at least, as much as I tell her—and why I've made the decisions I have. Why I'm thinking of leaving school and coming home for a while. Of course she'll understand.

Won't she?

The silence in the closed-up car was her only answer as she flipped on her blinker and slowed for the exit that would lead her home. It was the one place she wanted to be more than anywhere else at this very moment. It was also the one place that caused her heart to race with uncertainty as she considered the confrontation that was bound to come— sooner or later.

LAURA'S EYES WERE GRITTY and her stomach growled. She tore her gaze away from the computer screen and checked her watch. Three o'clock? How was that possible? She'd scarcely had any breakfast and had worked right through lunch, stopping only long enough to grab the iced tea, which she'd long since finished. It was no wonder she could never gain enough weight to erase what she considered her angular facial features and straight, boyish frame.

She shook her head. Mitchell used to scold her about getting so caught up in studies or work that she forgot to eat. If he were still alive today he'd have come in hours earlier and made her stop for lunch.

But he's not. And neither is Peter. They've been gone for almost ten years now—an entire decade. And they're not coming back, so quit wishing for something that will never happen. You'll see them again when your life here is over, and not before. So get on with what you need to do until then.

Shaking off the melancholy that threatened to overwhelm her, even after all this time, she headed for the kitchen, mentally running through her options for a quick meal. Surely there was enough for a sandwich of some sort. If not, she'd open a can of soup, pour it in a bowl, and heat it in the microwave. Either would be fine. And then she could get back to the pro-life article she was writing for the Christian women's magazine.

Can't imagine why these publications keep asking me to write for them, she thought as she sniffed the nearly empty package of lunch meat and then shuddered and tossed it into the garbage. *It sure isn't for my great writing style. There have got to be a whole lot of pro-life women out there who are better writers than I am, but I suppose it's my position as a doctor that gives me credibility.*

Having given up on the sandwich idea, she pulled a can of chicken soup from the cupboard, making a mental note to make a grocery run before the day was over. That was another point Mitchell had stressed with her in the early years of their marriage.

"We live in Colorado. It snows here in the winter—a lot. And sometimes it isn't convenient or even possible to make a last-minute grocery run. We really need to keep the kitchen stocked for emergencies, you know."

Yes, she had known. He was right, and she always meant to follow up. But then another project would come along and demand her attention, and once again such mundane things as the need to feed her family fell by the wayside.

It's a good thing Mitchell was practical and took care of what needed to be done around here to hold us all together. One of us certainly had to, or our children might have starved to death.

The reminder that her son had died despite Mitchell's practical nature punched a red-hot poker into her gut, but she pushed it away and opened the can of soup. Too bad she didn't have a few crackers to go with it, but she'd add that to the grocery list she now planned to make while she ate.

A noise from the front of the house jerked her back from her thoughts, and she frowned. She knew the wind was blowing, but she couldn't imagine that it had caused that much noise. Her heart skipped a beat as she put the can down and commanded her feet to take her toward the entryway.

"Hello?" she called, wishing her voice didn't reflect the uneasiness she felt.

"Mom?"

Laura felt her eyes widen.

"Megan? Is that you?"

Her daughter's familiar laugh melted the last of the tension in Laura's heart.

"Who else would be coming in your front door and calling you Mom?"

Who else, indeed? It was a question best ignored.

Laura stepped into the entryway as Megan closed the door behind her. Wrapped in a blue parka, her long curls appearing to explode from her head and fall down her back in an unruly tangle, the young woman pulling her roller suitcase behind her looked more like the teenager who had balked at starting high school than a self-assured medical student. Was that a flicker of fear Laura saw in her daughter's green eyes? If so, Megan quickly banished it, replacing it with a beaming smile that reached every corner of her face.

"I'm home early," she announced, letting go of the suitcase and dropping her shoulder bag on the small table beside the door.

Before Laura could think to ask why her daughter was home early, Megan enveloped her in a hug, the warmth of which seemed to flow directly down Laura's spine. Though many questions remained to be answered, for now the grateful mother would welcome her only remaining child, whatever the reason for her visit. Laura just wished she'd had the presence of mind to stock the kitchen with at least some basic food staples for just such an unexpected occasion as this.

Ah well, she thought, pulling back to smile into her daughter's lovely face, *we'll just order a pizza like we used to, and then sit around the kitchen table and eat it while we catch up on one another's news—whatever that may be.*

* * *

MEGAN HAD SCARFED DOWN her third piece of pizza when she noticed her mother was still picking at her first.

"Why aren't you eating, Mom? You adore pizza. And we got your favorite kind."

Laura smiled. "You're right. I really do love Canadian bacon and pineapple. And I should be hungry by now, since I forgot to stop for lunch."

Megan raised her eyebrows. "You forgot? Gee, what a surprise. That is so you, Mom. But you really have to stop that. You work too hard to be skipping meals. Besides, you're just way too skinny." She smiled and did her best to put a teasing tone into her voice. "I'm afraid if you turn sideways I'll lose you."

The joke seemed to be lost on her mother, and Megan realized that no matter how hard she tried to act natural and happy, the woman who gave birth to her knew something was up.

"Again, you're right, sweetheart. I know I should eat. In fact, just before you came I was about to heat a cup of soup."

"A cup of soup? An entire cup?" The teasing tone bordered on sarcastic now, as Megan continued. "Wow, Mom, do you think you could handle all that? I mean, knowing you, you probably didn't even eat breakfast today." She leaned forward and frowned as she studied her mother's expression. "You didn't, did you?"

Laura dropped her gaze before looking back up. "I'm afraid not. I did have some coffee, though—and some orange juice."

Megan shook her head. "You, the family doctor, always lecturing everyone else about taking care of themselves, and you can't even remember to eat. Seriously, Mom, you know better."

"Of course I do. And you're absolutely right. I'm setting a terrible example for others, especially you. It's just . . . I had this Skype meeting with some young medical students—women about your age—and they seemed so eager to hear why I'm pro-life. We had a great discussion. And then I had this article to work on."

As her mother talked about the magazine article, Megan felt her stomach rebel. No doubt she'd eaten more pizza than she should have, but something told her it was more than that.

"Um, Mom?" She reached across the small kitchen table and laid her hand on her mother's arm. "I need to tell you something."

Laura's monologue about her magazine article stopped midsentence. "I'm listening."

Megan took a deep breath. "Alex and I . . . broke up."

Sadness darted across her mother's face before it settled into her brown eyes. She nodded. "I wondered. You hadn't mentioned him lately. Is that why you came home early?"

"Sort of," Megan hedged. "I mean, yes, I suppose Alex is the reason I came today instead of waiting until next week for Thanksgiving."

Laura took Megan's hand in hers. "Did he . . . ? Was he the one who ended it?"

Megan hesitated, not trusting herself to answer. "Not . . . exactly," she said, hoping her mother would leave it at that.

"I'm so sorry, baby." She raised Megan's hand to her lips and kissed it. "You don't need to elaborate if you don't want to. But you're going to be OK. You know that, don't you?"

Megan nodded again. "I know," she whispered.

After a few seconds of silence that seemed to stretch into an eternity, Megan said, "There's more."

Laura raised her eyebrows.

"I'm . . . pregnant."

Megan watched her mother's eyes grow wide and then dim with realization. But at least the words had been spoken. No longer did she have to hold the secret inside. Now they could talk about it . . . and make plans.

The knot in Megan's stomach relaxed as relief washed over her.

Chapter 2

LAURA WASN'T SURE IF HER JAWS ACHED from forcing herself to smile or from clenching her teeth. It had been a long afternoon and evening, and she was relatively certain she'd done and said all the proper things in response to Megan's announcement. But what she'd really wanted to do was to race from the kitchen and lock herself in her room, put a pillow over her head, and wail to the heavens. That she'd had such a reaction, despite the fact that she hadn't acted on it, was nearly as distressing to her as Megan's bombshell itself.

And a bombshell it was. From the moment Megan walked in the front door, Laura suspected there was some sort of problem. But this? Her daughter pregnant? Now, at such a strategic point in her developing—not to mention, unmarried—life? No, Laura had not seen that coming. Not even a remote possibility. Megan had always had such a good head on her shoulders. She was mature and strong, with a clear sense of direction and high moral standards.

Or so Laura had thought. Suddenly she wasn't so sure. She'd only met Alex Williams a couple of times and had not realized how serious—or potentially destructive—their relationship might be. How could she have been so blind, so out of touch?

Then again, coming back to the Megan she thought she knew, why would Laura even consider such a thing?

Her daughter had always made a point of the fact that she planned to honor her mother's hard work and sacrifice to put her through school, and more than once had vowed never to be distracted from her goals. She'd also vowed to save herself for marriage.

"Quite obviously she broke both those vows," Laura whispered into the darkness, as she lay on her back on the still-made bed, staring up at an invisible ceiling. It had been awhile since she'd wished so passionately for Mitchell to be lying beside her. She could nearly feel the strength of his shoulder as she nestled up against him. How much easier it would be to absorb this shock and work through it if she had him to lean on, as she had in the beginning.

"But I don't, do I?" Tears bit her eyes and spilled over onto her face, dripping down into her ears. "You're my husband now, Lord. You're the One I need to lean on, the only One who can get me through this. I know You're there. I know You're listening. But it would help so much if I could just hear a word or two in return."

None came, and Laura closed her eyes, ignoring the tears that continued to dampen her ears, hair, and pillow. In that moment she felt like the biggest hypocrite imaginable, as the pro-life words she had spoken during her Skype meeting earlier that day came back to haunt her. "It's so easy when it's just a theory, when the problem hasn't invaded your own life, your own home. But now? Oh Father, I do *not* want this to be happening! I just want it all to go away, to go back to where we were yesterday, before Megan came home."

Continued silence surrounded her, even as she wondered what Megan was thinking at this very moment. Was she too lying in bed, crying? If so, was it for her lost love . . . or her lost dreams? Would she ever go on to become a doctor now, or was it more likely that she would take some lesser job out of necessity, some practical profession that would enable her to raise her child as a single parent?

Should I encourage her to try to reconcile with Alex? Is that even a possibility? And would I really want that for her—and for her baby? Is it better for a child to have two married parents, regardless of the quality of their character or relationship, than to be raised by one loving parent? I'm a single parent, after all. But not in the same way. I was married when Megan and Peter were born. How would I ever have survived those early years without Mitchell? She covered her mouth to muffle a sob. *How am I to survive without him now?*

She rolled over onto her stomach, burying her face in the already wet pillow, and gave herself over to her grief, as the losses of the past and those of the future merged together in her aching heart.

❊ ❊ ❊

A THIN WINTER SUN peeked through the early morning clouds as Megan moved as quietly as possible around the kitchen, making coffee and doing her best to ignore the queasiness in her stomach. Her morning sickness wasn't as severe as some cases she'd heard about, but it wasn't exactly a walk in the park either.

"You're up early."

Megan started at the sound of her mother's voice behind her. She turned, hoping her smile appeared genuine. "I tried not to wake you," she said, studying Laura's eyes. Their puffiness confirmed the muffled sobs Megan had heard during the night.

"You didn't. I had the alarm set. I need to be at the clinic by nine."

Megan nodded. She wasn't surprised that her mother was going to work today, but somehow she'd hoped for more time together.

"I made coffee," Megan offered. "Let me pour you a cup."

Laura's smile was strained. "That would be nice. Thank you, sweetheart."

"How about some eggs and toast? Or a bowl of cereal?"

Laura shook her head as she took a seat at the table. "Coffee is fine for now. You know I'm not much of a break-fast eater. Besides, you'd be hard-pressed to find any eggs or cereal in this house. If you want any breakfast this morning, it will probably have to be leftover pizza."

Megan's stomach roiled at the thought. "I'll pass. But I'll go to the store and stock you up on a few things while you're at work. You need to eat, Mom. How else are you going to keep your strength up?"

"You sound like your father. He was always saying things like that."

"He was right."

Laura sighed. "Fine. I'll stop on the way to the clinic and pick up some fruit or yogurt or something."

Megan set a steaming mug in front of her mother. "Promise?"

Laura looked up and raised her eyebrows. "I promise. Now what about you? What are you going to do today?"

"I thought I'd unpack a few things and then make that much-needed trip to the grocery store. Leftover pizza only lasts so long, you know. Maybe I'll fix something special for dinner so it'll be ready when you get home tonight."

Her mother's smile seemed a bit more relaxed this time. "That would be nice. I'd like that. I know how much you love to cook."

"Exactly. And I hardly ever get a chance to do it."

Megan settled into a chair next to Laura and nursed her own cup of coffee, wishing she had some flavored creamer to spruce it up a bit.

"So . . . you're going to unpack," Laura said. "I guess that means you're not heading back to school right away."

"Not much sense in it," Megan answered, setting her cup down. "I just thought, since the Thanksgiving holiday is next week anyway, I'd just stay over and go back the following Monday."

"So you do plan to go back to school then."

Megan frowned, pausing before she answered. "For the rest of the semester anyway. After that . . . I'm not so sure. I . . . I really haven't decided anything beyond that. I thought maybe we—you and I—could talk that through together."

Laura nodded. "Of course we can. And we will. I'm concerned about how all this is going to affect your education, your plans for . . . the future."

"I'm concerned about that too, Mom, believe me. Why do you think I came home early? I needed someone to talk to, to pray with, to bounce ideas off of. You're the only one I can trust to do that with. You know that, don't you?"

Laura nodded again, and Megan saw the glisten of tears in her eyes. "I do know that, sweetheart. And I appreciate it. This is definitely something we should work through together—with the Lord's help and guidance, of course."

"Absolutely."

"I do have one question, though."

Megan waited.

"It's about . . . Alex. You didn't say how he felt about all this."

Megan felt her shoulders droop and her stomach churn. "I didn't, did I?" She sighed, the question of how much to tell her mother once again pricking at her thoughts. "That's because he doesn't know. I didn't tell him. I . . . just didn't see any point in it. Not now anyway. I mean, it would be different if we were still . . . together. Of course I would have told him then. But now? It would seem like I was using our baby to try and trap him in some way." She shook her head, her golden red mane tossing in the process. "I've already made it perfectly clear to him that we're through, and I certainly don't want him thinking otherwise or feeling indebted to support me in some way. I truly don't, Mom. Besides, he's already moved on to someone else."

Laura reached out her hand and laid it on Megan's arm, warming her with the touch. "He still has a responsibility to you—and the baby."

Megan nodded. "I know. But . . . I'm just not ready to tell him yet. I need to figure out what I'm going to do first. Then I can think about letting him know. For now, it's enough that I can share this with you and know you're in my corner."

Laura's hand tightened on Megan's arm before she withdrew it and picked up her mug to take a sip.

❄ ❄ ❄

IT WAS FRIDAY MORNING and Alex Williams had a date with Chloe that night. He knew he should be excited about it, but after just a couple of weeks he was already growing bored with her. She was pretty, but she'd offered no challenge, giving herself to him on their second date. Instead of feeling victorious, Alex felt cheated. And now he couldn't stop thinking about Megan.

I made a big mistake, he thought as he trudged across the campus on the way to his first class. *Megan was more than just pretty. She was smart and fun—and completely pure, until I came along.* He grimaced, remembering how hard he'd had to work to get what he wanted from her—and how she'd cried afterward, saying she'd betrayed her mother, her faith, and herself. She also told him she'd never forgive him for what he'd done, but he thought sure she'd come around. After all, she'd wanted it too . . . hadn't she? So he'd nudged her a bit. Was that so bad? It wasn't like things hadn't been headed in that direction anyway.

What was I thinking? Megan was perfect for me. I loved being with her, and she has the same faith as my parents, even if mine isn't what it should be. Still, I wouldn't want to end up with someone who wasn't a Christian . . . would I?

The thought puzzled him and he frowned, kicking at a few stray leaves. If his parents' faith didn't matter enough to him to adopt it as his own, why did he care whether or not the girls he dated shared that faith? But though he had no logical answer for his own question, he knew it did matter, and Chloe didn't begin to measure up.

Megan. I really need to see you, to talk to you again, to see if we can put things back together. Surely you're not still mad at me, are you?

He pulled his cell phone from his pocket and let his finger hover over the speed dial button that would connect him to her phone. Would she answer? And if she did, would she even consider talking to him after what he'd done? After all, she'd told him in no uncertain terms that they were through. He also knew she'd seen him on campus with Chloe, and that certainly wasn't going to help his cause.

He shoved the phone back into his pocket. Class would start in five minutes. There wasn't enough time. He'd wait and call her later in the day. Maybe by then he'd figure out what to say.

Chapter 3

AFTER LAURA ARRIVED AT THE CLINIC and found herself greeted by a full waiting room, the morning had flown by. There was nothing like work to keep her mind from wandering into dark corners. Though she'd promised Megan to stop and pick up something to eat on the way in, she'd quickly forgotten her promise and had instead fueled her busyness with her daily dose of caffeine. Even lunch had come and gone before the feisty receptionist had alerted her to the time.

"Doctor, if you don't take a break right now, I'm going to have to kidnap you and drive you somewhere just to get you out of here."

Laura grinned in spite of herself. Bettina was a character, to say the least, but a good-hearted one—and a hard worker besides. However, the slightly overweight, middle-aged woman with the coffee-colored skin and warm brown eyes was not one to let rank or position intimidate her. She cared about people, period. Patients, doctors, nurses, homeless people who wandered in off the street looking for a handout, she treated them all the same—firmly and with no nonsense, but also with dignity and courtesy. And she never backed down when she believed she was right.

Bettina stood over Laura now, her hands on her hips and the twinkle in her eyes betraying her scowl. Still, Laura knew the woman wouldn't rest until the situation was remedied.

She sighed. "Fine. You're right. I probably do need a break. It's just that there are still so many people out there, waiting to be seen, and—"

"And Dr. Farmington will see them while you go to lunch." She snorted. "Lunch! It'll be dinnertime before you know it. Now get up out of that chair, put your coat on, and get out of this place for an hour, will you?" She shook her finger at Laura. "Don't make me follow through on my threat to kidnap you."

Laura laughed and shook her head as she stood to her feet. "I'm going, I'm going. I will not force you to kidnap me," she kidded. She reached for her coat and purse. "But I'm coming back as soon as I get something to eat. There are far too many patients for Dr. Farmington to handle on his own, especially at his age."

Bettina snorted again. "If you wait for us to run out of patients before you go home, you'll never get out of here. Now didn't you say your daughter came home yesterday? So what in the world are you doing here? Go home and spend some time with her. Dr. Farmington and I can handle things just fine around here. Go on, now."

Laura was still shaking her head as she buttoned her coat and headed for the door. As usual, Bettina was probably right. But Laura wasn't about to admit that out loud.

❈ ❈ ❈

THOUGH THE TEPID WINTER SUN offered little real warmth that afternoon, at least it wasn't snowing and the winds were calm. Laura decided it was the perfect time for a good, brisk walk. Why spend her time away from the office sitting in a closed-up restaurant somewhere when she could be out in the fresh air?

Snagging a sandwich from a nearby deli, she set out to make the most of her rare work break. Admittedly, if it hadn't been for Bettina's stubborn insistence, Laura would have continued working right up to the end of the day. But now that she'd been forced into a break, she had to admit that her stomach felt empty and her taste buds nearly drooled at the thought of biting into the ham and cheese on rye that awaited her.

After nearly fifteen minutes of traversing several downtown blocks, Laura spied a perfect landing spot. A small park with a handful of empty tables and benches appeared to be waiting just for her, so she settled into the one that seemed to get the most direct sunlight and then opened her sandwich and offered a quick prayer of thanks before diving in.

Delicious. I hadn't realized how hungry I was until now. I really need to get a better grip on this regular eating thing.

She smiled at the thought of Megan's admonition about doing just that. *So like Mitchell*, she thought, closing her eyes briefly to allow herself the poignant memory of her beloved husband. When Peter's face swam up to meet his father's, Laura quickly banished them both and opened her eyes, determined to finish her sandwich and get back to work.

With nagging thoughts of Megan's recent newsflash dancing around the peripheries of her consciousness, she swallowed the last bite of her late lunch before rising from the bench and depositing her trash in the nearby receptacle. It was time to head back to the clinic.

She'd gone less than two blocks when a familiar sign caught her eye: Jenny's Treasures. Laura smiled. She hadn't stopped in to see her friend in ages. Might she have time for a quick visit today?

She glanced at her watch and nearly decided to keep going, but a tug at her heart stopped her. Jenny wasn't getting any younger, and no one knew better than Laura how fragile life could be. It would do her good to reconnect with the elderly woman who insisted on running her little store herself, rather than hiring someone else to do it for her. Jenny's positive attitude and humor always warmed Laura's heart, though they often went months between visits.

Resolved not to let any more time go by, Laura pulled the door open and stepped inside to the sound of clanging bells, announcing her arrival.

"Be right there," came the voice from the back room.

In less than a minute the blue curtain that separated the shop from the office swooped open and Jenny stepped out. Laura smiled at the familiar sight. Despite Jenny's ever-multiplying wrinkles and her short white hair, the woman seemed ageless. The light that popped into her pale blue eyes at the sight of Laura only intensified that impression.

"Laura!" Jenny exclaimed, coming out from behind the counter and extending her arms in a welcoming hug. "I'm so glad you stopped by. I was thinking about you just the other day."

Laura nearly melted into Jenny's embrace, and she was surprised at the tears that stung her eyes. She blinked them away as quickly as they'd come and stepped back to look into her friend's smiling face.

"You look wonderful," Laura said. "You never change, do you?"

Jenny laughed, and the sound was melodic to Laura's ears. "Oh, my dear, if you're talking about my looks, I assure you I'm changing almost daily. This old body is wearing down, but my spirit is as young as ever." Her smile widened and she nodded toward the back room. "Come and sit with me for a moment and we'll catch up. Do you have time?"

Laura hesitated. "Not much, but a few minutes won't hurt. I still need to get back to work."

Jenny nodded as she led the way toward the curtain. "Still working, working, working." She clucked what Laura imagined was disapproval. "Now that's something that really hasn't changed. You really need to learn to slow down and smell the roses a little more."

Laura followed Jenny, past the vast array of lace doilies, Blue Willow china pieces, and various other assorted items that tugged nostalgically at her heart, behind the curtain and into the tiny room where everything from sewing and quilting, bookwork, and tea time took place. Though she'd only been back there a handful of times, she sighed at the familiarity of it.

"Bettina tells me the same thing," she said as they settled onto the too-soft couch against the back wall. "Well, maybe not in those word."

Jenny laughed. "I met Bettina once, remember? I can't imagine her ever saying anything about stopping to smell the roses, but I have no problem picturing her giving you advice—and in no uncertain terms."

Laura chuckled. "She did that today, as a matter of fact. Why do you think I'm out wandering around town in the middle of the afternoon? Besides, you and Bettina aren't the only ones trying to get me to slow down and take care of myself. Now I've got Megan at home, telling me the same thing."

Jenny raised her eyebrows. "Megan's home? Already? I would have thought she wouldn't be coming until Thanksgiving."

Laura felt a hot flush creep up her neck and into her cheeks. She really hadn't planned to mention Megan's visit—not yet anyway.

"She decided," Laura began, "to come home a few days early. It was a nice surprise, really."

"I imagine so," Jenny agreed. "Is everything going well with her at school?"

Laura swallowed before answering. "Just fine. I guess she wanted a few extra days off, since her grades are so good and all."

Jenny nodded. "Oh, yes, from what you've said in the past, that daughter of yours has a good, steady head on her shoulders. I'm not surprised she'd excel at school."

Laura opened her mouth to respond and then thought better of it when she spied a quilt lying on the end of the sofa where Jenny sat. "Something you're working on?" she asked, indicating the quilt with a nod of her head.

Jenny raised her eyebrows and then followed Laura's gaze. A smile spread across her face as she answered. "Ah, this is my Christmas quilt. I make one every year. Didn't I ever tell you that?" She lifted it carefully and held it up for Laura to see. "I'm almost done with it."

The beautiful designs, done in various shades of green and red, nearly took Laura's breath away. It was one of the most beautiful quilts she'd ever seen.

"I knew you sold quilts in the store, but no, you never mentioned your Christmas quilts. In fact, I had no idea you made any of these quilts yourself."

Jenny laughed again. "Oh, my dear, I certainly don't make them all. Just one each year, right in time for Christmas. And I don't sell it. It's a gift for someone special."

"What a wonderful idea! Who is it for this year?"

Jenny laid the quilt in her lap. "I don't know yet. I never know when I start working on it in the spring. I just pray as I stitch, and listen until God tells me what to do with it."

Laura reached out and gently touched the soft fabric on Jenny's lap. "I've never done any quilting myself." She looked up into Jenny's face. "I don't suppose that surprises you."

Jenny's eyes twinkled. "Not at all. You are far too driven to sit still for as long as it would take to put a quilt together." She smiled. "It's no small undertaking, you know. The stitching is really only a small part of the project. Capturing the heart of the story you want to tell is of utmost importance."

"Story?" Laura frowned. "There's a story in your quilts?"

"Absolutely. In fact, the story behind this Christmas quilt is one you may already know." She leaned forward slightly. "I'm basing it on the life of someone I greatly admire: Elizabeth Blackwell."

Laura felt her eyes widen. "The first woman doctor in our country?"

"Exactly. She was an amazing woman, and not just because of her accomplishments in medicine."

"There's more? As a woman physician, I know of the great strides she made for other women wanting to enter the field of medicine. And I know of her adamant opposition to abortion. But I'm afraid I don't know much else about her life. Should I?"

"Most definitely, my dear." Jenny smiled. "And I'd be more than happy to tell you about her if you're interested."

Suddenly aware of the time, Laura glanced at her watch. "I would love that. Really I would. But not today. I need to get back to the office. I've been gone too long already." She locked eyes with the older woman and spoke from her heart, surprising herself at the sincerity of her request. "I truly would like to hear her story, though. May I come back another time?"

Jenny laid her hand on Laura's. "Of course you can. You know I'm usually here, and the shop is seldom so busy that I can't break away for a cup of tea and a chat. Why don't you call ahead whenever you feel you can come by, and we'll lock in a time? Before this quilt is done, you shall have heard the entire story of this courageous woman."

"I'm looking forward to it," Laura said, meaning every word.

"As am I, my dear."

And with that Laura stood to her feet and allowed herself to be escorted to the front door.

MEGAN HAD SCARCELY HAULED THE LAST BAG of groceries into the house when her phone rang. Rummaging in her purse, she located it and pulled it out to glance at the caller name.

It wasn't at all who she'd expected. In fact, it was probably the last person on her possibility list. Her mother? That would have been her first guess, though the woman scarcely interrupted her work routine to make personal phone calls. Her roommate or one of her friends from school, calling to make sure she'd gotten home safely? Her second guess. Alex Williams? Never. They were through, weren't they? Of course they were. She had made that fact very clear to him. Besides, he was involved with someone else now.

She hesitated. What was the point of answering? She wasn't anywhere near ready to tell him about the baby—their baby. Even if she did, she had no idea how he might react. None of the likely scenarios played out well in her imagination.

No. This was not the time to risk a conversation with Alex. She was home where she belonged, working through her situation with her mother. Alex's involvement at this point, whatever that might amount to, would only muddy the waters.

She laid the phone on the counter, allowing the call to go to voice mail. Maybe she'd check the message later— maybe she wouldn't. Instead she concentrated on putting away the groceries and planning that special meal she'd mentioned to her mother. That was really the only thing she wanted to think about right now. Soon enough she'd be back at school, attending classes and writing papers, cramming for exams and dodging personal questions from anyone who dared to ask. Somehow she would make it through until the end of the semester. After that, until she and her mom had time to really work through all the possibilities, it was anyone's guess.

"Megan? I'm home."

Megan felt her eyes widen. Her mother had come home from work before dark? Unheard of! She smiled, knowing the early appearance was for her sake. Leaving the groceries in the sacks, she turned and waited.

"In here, Mom," she called. "I just got back from the store. I haven't started cooking yet."

Laura appeared in the kitchen doorway, her cheeks flushed, no doubt from the cold. She smiled as she unbuttoned her coat and tossed it over the back of one of the kitchen chairs. "That's perfect. We can work together—like the old days. We'll just cook up a storm and then eat until we pop. What do you think?"

Megan laughed. "I think that's the best idea I've heard all day. I hope you're up to lasagna because that's what I planned on when I went shopping. It might take a while, though, so we can munch on sourdough bread while we're cooking."

Laura pulled open the pantry door and retrieved a couple of aprons. "This makes it official," she said, tossing one to Megan. "Let the cooking begin!"

"Works for me," Megan responded, donning the apron. "Just one question: What in the world are you doing home before dark? I didn't expect you for hours."

Laura laughed. "You know me too well. But Bettina insisted I take off awhile this afternoon, so I went for a walk, grabbed a quick bite to eat, and ended up stopping at Jenny's Treasures. You remember that place?"

When Megan nodded and said she did, Laura continued. "Anyway, I visited with Jenny for a few minutes and then hurried back to the clinic. But when I got there both Bettina and Dr. Farmington insisted I go home. Since the patient load had miraculously shrunk in my absence, I took them up on the rare offer. And, well, here I am."

"I'm glad, Mom." Megan smiled. "This is exactly the sort of quality time I need to spend with you right now."

Laura nodded and slipped the apron over her head. "Well then, let's get busy. That lasagna is calling."

Chapter 4

ALEX RAN HIS FINGERS THROUGH HIS SHORT, dark hair, frustrated at the realization that he'd left a message for Megan nearly two hours earlier, and she hadn't even bothered to return his call. Had he really expected her to? Probably not, but he'd hoped. Still, the later it got, the less it looked like it would happen. How much longer should he wait? He didn't want to risk having Megan call while he was out with Chloe, but he sure didn't want to stay home all evening, waiting for a call that might not come. Chloe wasn't his first choice for a Friday night date, but she was better than nothing.

I'll give Megan one more call. Maybe she'll pick up this time. He punched the speed dial number for Megan, but this time it didn't even ring. The call went straight to voice mail. She had turned off her phone.

"Great," he growled, tossing his phone onto the bed and stuffing his arms into his jacket sleeves. *Just great. She doesn't return my messages and then turns her phone off. I guess I know where I stand. What was I thinking, trying to get back with her? Who needs her anyway?*

Snatching his car keys from the desk beside the bed, he turned on his heel and headed for the door. Megan wasn't the only woman in the world. For tonight, Chloe would do— and then he'd get busy looking for a more suitable replacement. Chicks were a dime a dozen, right? There was no reason to get all worked up over one of them when there were so many others out there, just waiting for Alex Williams to give them some of his valuable time.

Smiling, he nearly believed what he'd said to himself as he headed down the stairs toward the parking lot. He would have a good time tonight, with or without Miss Megan Branson.

* * *

IT WAS PAST MIDNIGHT and Megan hadn't slept a wink. Her sheets and blankets were in a jumble, and she'd punched and fluffed her pillow so many times she'd lost count. Should she just give up and turn on the light and read or something?

Or something.

She knew what that something was that called her. It was the unheard message on her voice mail, no doubt from Alex since she hadn't answered or returned his call earlier. She'd managed to keep the nagging thought at bay throughout the late afternoon and evening hours as she and her mother cooked and ate and cleaned up afterward, somehow getting through the entire event without once mentioning the elephant in the room.

A tiny elephant to be sure, she thought, laying her hand on her still-flat stomach. *But growing all the time. It won't be long until my secret will be out. Even Alex will know, whether I tell him or not. For a guy who's already involved with someone else, I can't imagine how trapped he'll feel to learn he's going to be a father.*

Then again, does he even have to know? If I leave school at the end of the first semester, I won't be showing yet—at least not that much..

Her thoughts veered off toward school itself then. Why wasn't she more upset at the idea of leaving school, even if only for a short time? She'd had her future mapped out for her—until now. She was undoubtedly going to have to take a detour, one way or the other, to resolve this issue. Giving up medical school completely shouldn't even be one of the options, yet she realized it might be. And somehow it didn't devastate her as she believed it should.

She shook her head, as if to clear her mind of these thoughts. Back to the immediate issue—Alex. Did she really have to tell him at all? It was a tempting thought, one that was at least a distinct possibility. What good could come of involving Alex in the baby's life? It isn't as though he'd be thrilled and want to be an active participant . . . would he? And even if he did, could she handle having him around after what he'd done?

No. She'd allowed herself to have a terrible lapse in character judgment with Alex—not to mention a complete failure of discernment about setting safe boundaries in their relationship. Not to mention that she'd gotten caught up in feelings of infatuation, confusing them with real love! What was the point of compounding her existing errors?

Her cell phone lay on the stand next to the bed, silently nagging her to at least check the message. After all, it wasn't as if she had to return the call. All she had to do was listen.

She sighed. It was obvious she wasn't going to get any sleep until she did. Snatching the phone from its resting place, she punched the number to retrieve her messages. And then she waited, scarcely breathing.

Just as she'd thought, her only message was from Alex, and it certainly wasn't what she had expected to hear.

He wanted to talk to her. He missed her and knew he'd made a terrible mistake, but couldn't she forgive him and get past that somehow? Could they meet somewhere? They needed to talk, to try to work things out. Would she please call him back?

Her heart raced as emotions warred inside her. She despised the part of herself that, despite the way he'd treated her, still longed to return his call and, yes, even consider getting together to talk. But she wasn't so naïve as to think he would have left her such a message if he knew about the baby.

What's wrong, Alex? Is your new relationship not working out the way you expected, and now you want me back? Back for what? So you can hurt and humiliate me again? Do you really think I'm foolish enough to come back for seconds?

Ashamed of herself for her sarcastic tone, she asked the Lord to forgive her, then she pressed the erase button to delete the message. If Alex's ego was bruised and his new relationship faltering, he would just have to find some other way to remedy the problem. And with that she rolled over, determined to get some sleep at last.

❅ ❅ ❅

JENNY HAD BEEN PLEASANTLY SURPRISED when Laura called her midmorning on Saturday and asked if she could drop by during her lunch break. From the moment Jenny had spotted her younger friend standing just inside the door to the shop, she sensed this was no random visit. Divine fingerprints dusted the entire event, and the fact that a woman as busy and driven as Dr. Laura Branson would make a return visit the very next day confirmed it. Whatever God had in mind, Jenny knew it would be good.

"I can only stay a little while," Laura explained when she arrived. "Is this a good time?"

"It's the perfect time," Jenny said, smiling as she turned the Open sign to Closed in the front window. "I need a lunch break too, you know, so why not now? Come on in, my dear. I made tea, and I have scones to go with it."

"Oh, I didn't mean for you to go to any trouble," Laura protested as they settled into their seats on the worn couch.

"Really, it's enough that you're willing to give me some of your time to tell me Dr. Blackwell's story. You certainly don't need to worry about feeding me too."

Jenny laughed as she poured tea into the cups on the rich mahogany coffee table in front of them. "I love doing this. I seldom have anyone to share my tea with, and this is a real treat. Besides, my dear, you really could use a little more meat on your bones."

Laura rolled her eyes. "You too? It seems everyone is bound and determined to slow me down and fatten me up these days. Well, I'll have you know that Megan and I made lasagna last night, and I ate until I thought I'd burst. What do you think of that?"

"I think that's wonderful. I haven't had homemade lasagna in years."

Laura raised her eyebrows. "Well, then, I'll just bring some with me on Monday." She paused, her eyebrows returning to their normal position. "That is, if you don't mind my coming by again so soon."

Jenny set the teapot down on the trivet in the middle of the table and then laid her hand on Laura's. "It would be an answer to prayer for me. With all my family either gone on to heaven or moved halfway across the country, I get more than a little lonely these days. Why do you think I come into the shop every day? At least it gives me someone to chat with on occasion. And having a friend drop by regularly to share lunch with me? What a joy!" She patted Laura's hand. "You just feel free to come by as often as you can break away. Besides, that will give me something to look forward to between now and Monday—another visit with you, and lasagna besides."

A pang of what appeared to be regret or concern skittered across Laura's face. "I'd come tomorrow, but it's Sunday. I always go to church on Sunday morning, and now, with Megan home, we'll probably go out to eat afterward."

"I go to church on Sunday mornings too," Jenny assured her. "And it's the one day each week that I don't open the shop, so Monday is perfect. Meanwhile, what would you like to know about Dr. Elizabeth Blackwell?"

Laura seemed to consider the question before answering. "You said there was a lot more to her life than simply her medical accomplishments—though those were many, I know. What else can you tell me about her?"

Jenny picked up the quilt from the arm of the sofa and peered down at it. "I suppose, if you really want to know about the entire woman, we should start at the beginning, don't you agree?"

When she looked up, Laura's eyes were locked on hers, and she nodded. "Yes. That makes the most sense."

Jenny nodded. "All right, then." She fingered a patch in the middle of the quilt, filled with what appeared to be a bright red baby rattle, tied in a bow. "This patch represents Elizabeth's arrival in the world. As you may already know, although she's famous for being the first woman doctor in America, she was actually born in Bristol, England, on February 3, 1821. Her parents, Samuel and Hannah, were concerned because she was so weak and tiny at birth that they weren't sure she'd make it. They'd already lost a baby son a year earlier, so they were very cautious about introducing her to the rest of the family. They didn't even let her two older sisters see her until they felt she was doing better. Little did they know that the tiny girl who would never grow taller than five foot one would prove herself a giant as a pioneer in the medical field."

Jenny watched as Laura laid the remainder of her scone on the plate in front of her, her eyes downcast. "I suppose I never thought of Dr. Blackwell as an infant," she said before lifting her gaze. "But of course we all start out that way, don't we?"

Jenny smiled. "We certainly do, my dear. And none of us knows what the good Lord has in mind for our future. But we do know that whatever His plans for us, they are good."

Laura nodded, picking up her cup and sipping the now lukewarm liquid.

"More tea?" Jenny asked.

Laura looked up to meet Jenny's eyes. "No thank you. In fact, I really need to get back to the clinic."

"Already? Why, we've barely begun to dig into Elizabeth's young life."

Laura looked apologetic. "I know. And there's nothing I'd like better than to stay here all afternoon and continue our discussion. But I'm afraid I can't." Her eyes lit up as she smiled. "But we can certainly pick up where we left off when I return on Monday—leftover lasagna in hand."

"It's a date," Jenny said, pleased at the prospect. "But before you go, may we have a quick word of prayer together?"

For a moment, Laura appeared puzzled. Then her face relaxed and she reached out to take Jenny's outstretched hands. "I would like that very much," she said, as she closed her eyes and bowed her head.

Chapter 5

THE SUN STILL SHONE ON SUNDAY, though predictions of a storm by midweek loomed. Laura's emotions were jumbled. She was relieved that her daughter was already home and wouldn't be driving from college in bad weather, but she couldn't deny that she was deeply disturbed over Megan's reason for returning early.

A baby, she thought, as she exited the church with Megan at her side. *Why can't I get used to the idea? That means I'll be a grandmother. What's so bad about that?*

She suppressed a sigh as she fumbled in her purse for the car keys. Admittedly, if the circumstances were different—meaning, if Megan were already through school and married—Laura would be thrilled. But there had been no wedding, nor did Laura expect there would be one any time soon, and her daughter's future in medicine was now up for grabs. Megan would undoubtedly join the ranks of single mothers, with all the accompanying limitations and challenges. To imagine she could still complete medical school and launch her career in the way Laura had planned for her daughter to do for so many years now seemed doubtful at best.

The question that those plans were more Laura's than Megan's niggled at her mind, but Laura pushed it away and tried to pull herself back from negative thoughts to instead focus on this morning's sermon. In preparation for the upcoming Thanksgiving holiday, the pastor had spoken on the importance of having a grateful attitude, regardless of circumstances. Laura had smiled and nodded, as she always did, but her heart refused to cooperate. Though she wished desperately to deny it, Laura knew she was not at all grateful about this new turn of events in her daughter's life, nor in hers, though she had no idea what to do to remedy the situation.

"So what do you think, Mom?"

Megan's voice jarred Laura back to the present, and she nearly dropped her keys in the process. She stopped in the middle of the parking lot and looked back at her daughter.

"What do I think about what?"

Megan appeared surprised. "About what we talked about this morning. I asked if we could pick up some sandwiches or something and go eat them in the Garden of the Gods. You know how much I love that place, and we haven't gone there together in quite a while. You said it depended on the weather." She glanced upward and shrugged before returning her gaze to Laura. "The sun's out, it's not windy, and we have warm coats. I say we go for it. But it's your call, Mom."

Laura hesitated. She too enjoyed visiting the Garden of the Gods on the west side of town. When the children were young, she and Mitchell used to take them there regularly, whether for picnics or climbing during the day or to sit on a rock outcropping in the evening and watch the sun set over the mountains. There really wasn't any excuse for not going there today. The weather was decent, and there probably wouldn't be many more opportunities to picnic outside before spring, so why not?

She smiled. "Sure, let's do it. We'll stop at that great little deli in Manitou Springs on the way. Sounds like a wonderful idea. I'm glad you thought of it."

Megan returned her smile. "Me too. Let's go. You want me to drive?"

Laura handed her the keys, and within moments they were heading for Colorado Avenue and the old part of town. Bare-limbed trees greeted them as they drove the familiar route past mostly two-story houses with wide porches, many with "room for rent" signs in the windows. Laura remembered how thrilled she and Mitchell had been when they bought their first house in this very neighborhood. *Two bedrooms, one bath, but with a basement that became a great playroom for the kids, especially in the winters. We didn't have much in those early days, when I was still in medical school and we were living on Mitch's sales commissions, but we were never happier.*

The thought darted into her mind then that it was only a few years later, not long after she had started working at the clinic, when she received the worst possible phone call. Her world as she'd known it shattered at that moment and left her adrift to care for Megan on her own.

She glanced sideways at her daughter. The girl was a young woman now. But was she ready to be a mother? True, becoming a single mother didn't necessarily preclude Megan's completing her education and also becoming a doctor. But would she? Would the baby change everything Laura had dreamed and worked for all these years since Mitchell and Peter died?

And what of Megan's relationship with the Lord? That she had compromised her long-held standards and lost her virginity reflected at least some sort of compromise in her relationship with the Him as well.

She sighed and turned to gaze out the passenger-side window. She would certainly pray about Megan's walk with the Lord, and broach the subject soon if Megan herself didn't do so. But as for her daughter's future, only time would tell, and Laura wasn't sure she wanted to know the answer.

※ ※ ※

ALEX WAS BUMMED. His Friday night date with Chloe had been everything he'd expected—physical and meaningless. What bugged him most about it was that it hadn't been that long ago when he would have considered it the perfect evening. Now it left him feeling empty and wanting more. Thoughts of the many hours he'd spent in church while growing up teased his memory, but he shoved them away, determined that his parents' religion wasn't going to interfere with his fun.

He'd tried to drown the thoughts and feelings by spending most of Saturday with his buddies, drinking beer and watching college football. Chloe had called twice, but he hadn't bothered to answer—hadn't even listened to her messages. No doubt she wanted to see him again before the weekend was over, but once was enough for him. He'd catch up with her one day next week—unless he had a better offer.

Which doesn't look like it's going to come from Megan, he thought, dragging himself from bed and hoping he'd find a couple of aspirin left inside the bottle in the medicine cabinet. *I've left her three messages, and still nothing.*

He peered in the mirror over the sink. Bloodshot eyes, topped with bedhead, looked back at him. He sighed and opened the medicine cabinet. It was obvious the moment he picked up the aspirin bottle that it was empty.

Great. Now I've got to get dressed and find a store open so I can get something for this pounding headache.

He slammed the medicine cabinet door shut and winced at the bang that echoed between his ears. *Maybe a shower will help. Then out to get some aspirin and coffee.* He reached inside the shower and turned the handle, waiting until steam emanated from the stall before climbing inside. If he could just pull himself together until he looked and felt presentable again, maybe he'd take a chance and head on over to Megan's dorm room. It was obvious she wasn't going to return his call and he hadn't succeeded in crossing paths with her during classes, so he'd have to find her and confront her in person. He just hoped he wasn't too late.

❋ ❋ ❋

MEGAN EASED HER MOM'S NEARLY NEW four-wheel drive Volvo off the road and onto a level spot near a large, low rock with a flat top, tailor-made for sitting and picnicking. Despite the fact that Megan drove an economical "green" car, she had to admit she was glad her mom chose something so safe and practical for the weather and terrain in that part of the country. It might be a bit more spendy than some cars, but the safety factor justified it.

Megan glanced up again at the rock she'd spotted for their picnic, set against the rich red earth that dominated the landscape. She was sure her still agile mother would have no problem climbing the few feet necessary to perch atop it, and besides, the location was perfect. They'd have a bird's-eye view of Cheyenne Mountain while they ate, and they'd be in just the right spot to catch the noonday rays besides.

"How's this?" she asked, putting the car in park and turning toward her mom.

Laura smiled. "Perfect. I couldn't have found a better place if I'd tried."

Megan exited the vehicle and opened the back door to retrieve their lunch. By the time she'd hit the alarm button to secure the car, Laura was already beginning the short climb to the top of the rock. Megan watched her, smiling. Her mother might be thin, but she certainly wasn't frail in any way. Megan admired her strength and stability, and was reassured that she could lean on it now, when she needed it most. Though her mother had always been uncompromising in her moral standards, Megan had never known her to be judgmental or condemning. Still, there were limits to what she could tell her mother about her situation—at least for now.

In moments she had scrambled up the rock behind her mother, and they both settled down with their lunch spread out between them. "Turkey and Swiss on rye," Megan commented, "with a dill pickle on the side." She looked up from her sandwich to Laura. "My favorite."

Her mother nodded. "I know. Mine too—most of the time. Though I like their shaved ham too." She chuckled. "Come to think of it, there isn't much at that little Manitou deli that I don't like."

Megan's heart warmed. This was just the sort of camaraderie she had hoped for with her mother. She was pleased that her mom hadn't beaten the pregnancy drum nonstop since Megan told her the news . . . though she was a bit concerned that she hadn't mentioned it much at all. It was the most drastic change to hit them since losing half their family in a car accident ten years earlier. Sooner or later, the two women would have to discuss the situation at length and decide what to do next.

But not today, Megan told herself, turning her eyes toward the distant mountains, deliberately zooming past the increasing influx of cars and tourists winding through the canyon road below, looking for their own picnic and climbing spots. *Today I just want to enjoy all this beauty. I'd almost forgotten how much I love it here. I'm so glad I decided to leave school and come home a few days early. I really needed this.*

The vibration of her cell phone in her jacket pocket interrupted her thoughts, but she ignored it, glad she'd turned off the ringer. She knew who it was, and she wasn't about to let Alex interrupt her enjoyable afternoon with her mother. She would have to deal with him sooner or later, but today was definitely not the time.

Chapter 6

"WHAT DO YOU MEAN, SHE'S NOT HERE?"

Alex's head still throbbed, and he seemed to be making no progress at all with Megan's roommate.

"I mean," the maddening young woman repeated, her earbuds hanging on a black wire around her neck and emanating a pulsating sound, "she is *not* here. No longer at school. Gone."

Alex scowled. "Gone? How can she be gone?"

The tall blonde rolled her eyes. "She packed a suitcase, got in her car, and left. Look, Alex, I don't mean to be rude, but I've got things to do, OK? I really don't have time to stand here and try to explain this to you. Besides, why should I? You two broke up, right? You're no longer an item, so she owes you no explanations about where she is—and neither do I."

He stopped the door just before she closed it in his face. "Fine," he said, struggling to pull up every ounce of restraint. "You're right. Neither of you owes me an explanation. But, seriously, I just want to talk to her. I *need* to talk to her."

The girl, who Alex had once thought attractive and now couldn't imagine why, nor could he remember her name, glared at him. "So call her."

"I did. Several times. She didn't answer and she hasn't called me back."

"Well, there you go. You may want to talk to her, but it's obvious she doesn't want to talk to you. And to be honest, neither do I."

She stuck the earbuds back in her ears and this time succeeded in closing the door before Alex could stop her. He considered knocking and trying again, but it was pointless. He may as well just give up and hope Megan would eventually turn up or call him back.

He started down the walkway toward his car, which he'd driven here straight from the drugstore where he'd purchased his much-needed aspirin. *Wait a minute. She packed a suitcase. That means she planned to be gone for several days. I haven't heard any rumors about her seeing anyone else, so it's not like she took off for some romantic weekend with a new boyfriend or something. Besides, that wouldn't be like her. So that means there's only one other place she could be—home. But why, with Thanksgiving just a few days away? Of course she'd go home then, but why now?*

Still frowning and shaking his pounding head, he climbed into his car and leaned back against the seat. Eyes closed, he tried to imagine what possible scenarios could have blasted Megan away from her studies just days before a holiday break. There weren't many. The only one he could think of was some sort of family emergency. Maybe her mom was sick or something. That might explain why Megan hadn't returned his calls. It also might mean that sooner or later she'd check her messages and respond. He sure hoped so. And he hoped it wouldn't take long. If there was one thing Alex Williams was not, it was patient.

He jammed the key into the ignition, started the car, and backed out of the parking spot. As much as he hated the thought, he knew he had to get back to his room and crack his own books. His parents would be none too happy with him if he messed up any worse than he already had. And if he flunked out of school or got into any serious trouble, his dad had already told him he'd have to get a job and start paying his own way. The idea did not appeal to Alex at all. He wasn't really qualified to get anything more than a menial job—which meant he'd never enjoy the finer things in life that being a doctor could bring him. It was the only reason he'd entered medical school, though he'd had no idea how grueling the schedule would be. There were times he wanted nothing more than to bale and go back home, where his mom fixed him three squares and he could go out and party with his friends whenever he wanted—so long as his parents didn't find out, of course.

But that was no longer an option, he reminded himself. So like it or not, he aimed his car back in the direction of his room where his books waited on the desk next to his bed. It would be a long and boring Sunday afternoon, but maybe— just maybe—Megan would surprise him with a phone call before nightfall.

❊ ❊ ❊

MEGAN WAS RESTLESS. Though it had been a pleasant Sunday, including church, the picnic at Garden of the Gods, and a quiet evening at home, she was beginning to wonder at her mother's reaction—or lack thereof—to her news. It wasn't as if Megan was anxious to discuss it, but the problem wouldn't go away if they ignored it.

She sighed and pulled out the chair in front of the desk where she'd spent so many hours poring over homework in high school. There was a certain comfort at being in these familiar surroundings, but she also felt as if she were running from reality.

Studies, she reminded herself, settling into her chair and picking up a heavy medical book. *I may not be at school, but that doesn't mean I can slack off. Mom and I have both invested far too much already to let all this slip away.*

She paused. *Mom and I . . .*

The all too familiar question of whose dream it was that she follow in her mother's footsteps and become a doctor danced close to her thoughts, but she shoved it down once again. She found the place in her studies where she'd left off a few days earlier and began to read. Her mind would not cooperate.

What if it does all slip away? What if all the time and effort and expense that have gone into my education end up being wasted? It would break Mom's heart.

She shifted gears then and thought of the child growing within her. *Not a fetus*, she reminded herself. *A baby. Mom has taught me that for years, and deep down I know she's right. I just wish this hadn't happened—not now, not yet.*

A wave of shame washed over her, as she thought of the many years her mother—and her dad too, before he died—had taken her to church and Sunday School, not to mention modeling a godly life in front of her and instilling in her a strong sense of right and wrong. So many of her friends from college dismissed such guidelines as something akin to ancient mythology, certainly not relevant in today's world. But Megan couldn't get past the idea that absolutes existed, in fact did not change, despite current cultural trends. What must her mother think of her now?

Her blinking cell phone caught her eye, as it lay on the edge of the desk beside her. She still hadn't done anything about contacting Alex. Why should she? He was the one who had violated her trust, who forced her to end their relationship. Still, it would be so much easier to move on if she weren't pregnant.

She shook her head. Wishing the baby away wouldn't change anything. She had allowed herself to get into a situation that left her vulnerable, and now she was paying the price. The only thing she could do about it at this point was to try to make the right decisions from this day forward. And she would need her mother's input for that to happen.

Megan forced her attention back to her book. She would allow this pleasant day to end on that same positive note, but tomorrow evening, when her mom returned from work, Megan would insist they discuss the situation. Until then, she must plow ahead with her studies.

❄ ❄ ❄

THE WEATHER WAS CHANGING, and not for the better.

Unless you're a snow bunny who thrives on the cold, Laura reminded herself. *Since I don't qualify, even after all my years of living here, I guess I'd better hurry before those clouds cut loose and start dumping flurries on my head.*

Bettina and Dr. Farmington had both seemed pleasantly surprised when Laura voluntarily opted to take a lunch break at noon on Monday. Then, instead of walking to Jenny's Treasures, Laura had hopped into her car and steered straight to the shop. She was disappointed when she had to park nearly a block away, and shivered as she clutched her bag containing the leftover lasagna and nearly raced for the front door. The warmth that radiated from inside as she entered was a delightful welcome.

Jenny stood behind the counter, ringing up a purchase for the only customer in the store. Laura admired the vast assortment of delicate pieces of antique jewelry and collectibles while she waited. At last the woman received her change and exited the shop, package in hand, smiling at Laura as she passed by.

"You're here," Jenny announced, beaming as she came toward her. After a quick hug she turned the window's Open sign to Closed, flipped the lock on the door, and beckoned for Laura to follow. "I'll put the tea on. Is that the promised lasagna in your bag?"

"It is," Laura said, following her friend behind the curtain. "I believe I remember that you have a microwave."

Jenny laughed. "Of course I do. I may be old, but I know a good invention when I see one. Microwave ovens are at the top of my good invention list."

Laura smiled and unwrapped her offering. In moments the tea was poured, the reheated lasagna was scooped out onto paper plates, and the two women had settled down on the soft couch.

"It smells delightful," Jenny exclaimed after offering a brief prayer of thanks for the food. "I haven't had homemade lasagna in . . . well, far too long, I'm afraid."

"This is the first time for me in a long time too," Laura admitted. "It was actually Megan's idea. She loves to cook."

The mention of Megan stirred Laura's memory of their brief exchange that morning. Her daughter seemed anxious to talk with her, but Laura had explained her need to get to the clinic early. She knew Megan would be waiting for her when she returned that evening, and no doubt they'd have to discuss what to do about the baby situation. Laura knew too that her daughter would be looking to her for answers—or, at least, for guidance and direction. How many times over the years had Laura given such advice to young women, never hesitating to lay out everything scripturally, to offer to pray, and to feel confident that she had done the right thing? So why was it so different this time? Why did she resist the very idea of discussing Megan's future at this point? The two had never had a problem talking about anything before, even during Megan's slightly difficult teen years. They had remained close, regardless of what came along, and Laura knew her child respected her opinion and valued her input.

And yet the wall of resistance toward discussing the situation had started to build the moment Megan told her of her pregnancy, and it was growing taller by the moment. What was wrong with her that she wasn't willing to address the issue?

"This is delicious," Jenny said, interrupting Laura's thoughts. "Every bit as good as it smells, and then some. That daughter of yours is quite a cook."

Laura nodded. "Yes, she is, isn't she?" She forced a smile.

"So," Jenny said, laying down her fork, "are you ready for more of Dr. Blackwell's story?"

Laura felt a surge of excitement. "I am. Very much so. I've been looking forward to it since Saturday."

Jenny smiled. "Then you shall have it. It's a story I so enjoy telling to any who will listen."

Lasagna temporarily forgotten, Laura sank back against the sofa's back and waited. She still wasn't clear why hearing Dr. Blackwell's story was so important to her right now; she only knew it was, and she wanted to absorb every word.

"As I believe I told you on Saturday, Elizabeth was a tiny, frail baby, and her parents questioned if she'd even survive. But survive she did, surprising them all with her determination and drive."

Jenny smiled and took a sip of her tea. "Her two older sisters were very much like their lively, outgoing mother, even sporting her brunette curls. Elizabeth, on the other hand, was much more her 'daddy's girl.' Physically, she had his coloring—gray eyes and pale blonde hair—and personality-wise, she resembled him as well. Both were perfectionists and often appeared stern, simply because they were so determined to press ahead to accomplish their goals, whatever they might be. But despite her natural tenacity, Elizabeth was a shy child, so much so that her father christened her Little Shy, a name that seemed at odds with her future accomplishments."

Laura raised her eyebrows. She had never heard the nickname applied to this famous woman doctor before. It was difficult to imagine that someone who was naturally shy could have accomplished so much.

"Elizabeth's family, including her siblings—there were eventually nine in all—quickly came to know her as the most persistent one in their clan. When the rest of them might be tempted to give up on something, Little Shy dug in and stuck with it until she succeeded. In fact, one day when was only six years old, she overheard her two older sisters discussing what they wanted to do and be when they grow up. Elizabeth immediately announced that she didn't yet know what she would be, but she did know it would be something hard."

Jenny set her cup down and leaned closer to Laura. "Quite prophetic, wouldn't you say?"

"It certainly was," Laura agreed, watching Jenny retrieve her fork and go after another bite of lasagna. Mulling over what she'd learned about Elizabeth "Little Shy" Blackwell, Laura followed suit and resumed eating her lunch.

Chapter 7

LAURA PLOWED through the busy afternoon with her usual dedication, though she couldn't dispel the surprising revelation that Dr. Elizabeth Blackwell, one of Laura's most admired heroines, was considered shy. Laura had never wrestled with that trait, and it was difficult to imagine someone who did still pushing on to achieve so much.

She'd just finished with her last patient of the day and was writing up a final report when Bettina knocked and then stepped into her tiny office, not waiting for Laura's invitation.

"You about done for the day?"

Laura looked up at the stocky, middle-aged woman with the short cropped dark hair and laughing eyes that betrayed her sometimes disapproving scowl.

"I am," Laura said, setting her pen on the desk. "How about you?"

Bettina shrugged. "You know me. I'm always ready to head home." She grinned. "Especially tonight. It's Earl's turn to fix dinner. And let me tell you, that man can cook."

Laura chuckled. "You've mentioned that before, but I'm still waiting for an invitation to try it for myself."

Bettina's eyebrows shot up. "Well now, we'll just have to fix that, won't we? Especially now that your daughter's home for a few days. Tell you what. We have a feast planned for

Thursday that'll fill you up till Christmas. Why don't the two of you come and join us?"

Laura felt her cheeks warm. "Oh Bettina, that's so sweet of you, but really, I wouldn't think of intruding on a family holiday like Thanksgiving. Megan and I will fix a small turkey at home that day, and then eat leftovers for the rest of the weekend until she goes back to school."

If she goes back to school.

The thought slipped unbidden into her mind, but she shook it away. Of course Megan would go back. Why wouldn't she? After all, she'd already indicated her desire to complete the semester, and then they'd figure it out from there.

Bettina planted her fists on her ample hips. "Intrude? You think you and Megan would be intruding to come to our house for Thanksgiving dinner?"

She shook her head. "You just don't get it, do you? If you'd be intruding, do you think I'd invite you in the first place? Listen, there is nothing my Earl likes better than cooking, especially since he took his early retirement from the city. He thrives on it—the more, the merrier, he always says. So trust me, you'd be doing him a favor to come on over and join us on Thursday. What do you say?"

Laura found herself wanting to say no, but couldn't really think of a believable reason. She'd already admitted that she and Megan had no plans other than eating home alone together, though the thought had crossed her mind earlier that day that perhaps they should invite Jenny to join them.

"I'd really like to, but my friend Jenny might end up being alone on Thanksgiving. You've met Jenny, the woman who runs Jenny's Treasures."

Bettina laughed. "Of course I've met her—only once, but I remember her well. And we'd love to have her come."

Laura hesitated. "Well, OK. But you really must let us bring something."

"Besides your appetites? OK, fine. Bring a dessert. We can never have too many of those."

The decision seemed to have been made, so Laura nodded. "All right. Thank you, Bettina. I know Megan will enjoy baking something special. What time should we come?"

"We'll eat around five or six o'clock," Bettina said, beaming now, "but you can come way before that. The family will start showing up by noon, and we'll have plenty of snacks to keep everyone busy until dinner. And when you come to our house, you *are* family. Just show up, ready to eat and have fun."

Laura nodded again. "All right. We'll be there. And thank you again."

Bettina turned, and Laura watched her leave the room. She supposed she'd better spring the news on Megan as soon as she got home that evening. It might even steer the conversation away from her daughter's personal situation, though Laura doubted that very much. What bothered her most was her own resistance to tackling the topic. Putting it off wouldn't make it go away, but she simply wasn't ready to deal with it quite yet.

❄ ❄ ❄

"HOW WAS THE LEFTOVER LASAGNA?" The question had occurred to Megan earlier in the day, and now she gave voice to it as she and her mom worked together at the kitchen counter to build a salad for dinner. "You must have been awfully hungry to take so much with you to work this morning."

Laura paused from her task. "You noticed how much lasagna I took?"

Megan laughed. "It's not like there wasn't enough left for me or anything. But yes, I did notice because you're usually not a big eater. In fact, I was surprised you remembered to pack a lunch at all. I usually expect you to work right through mealtime."

"You're right," Laura admitted, going back to slicing tomatoes. "I often do, I'm afraid. But lately I've been . . . " She paused, while Megan waited, watching her and wondering at the reason for her mother's hesitation. When Laura continued, she kept her gaze on the cutting board in front of her. "Lately I've been meeting with a friend at lunch. I thought it would be nice to share some of your delicious lasagna with her."

"And did she like it?"

Laura looked up and smiled. "She loved it. Why wouldn't she? It's wonderful."

"So who is this friend? Anyone I know?"

"Actually, yes, though not well. It's Jenny, the owner of Jenny's Treasures."

"Oh, sure, I remember her. You're right. I don't know her well, but the few times I met her she seemed really sweet."

"She is." Laura scraped the sliced tomatoes into the salad bowl, adding a red contrast to the green lettuce and cucumbers.

"So, Mom, how did all this come about? I mean, it's not like you to take off from work and spend time with friends, though I'm glad to know you're doing that for a change. It's good for you."

Laura shrugged. "Oh, I don't know. I was walking by the shop a few days ago and thought I should stop in and say hello. I did. And, well, we started talking and she invited me back and that's about all there is to it, I suppose."

Laura picked up a grater with one hand and a carrot with the other. "There's something else I need to tell you, Bettina invited us to join them for Thanksgiving dinner."

Megan stopped slicing mushrooms and gave her full attention to her mother. "And? Did you accept?"

"I did. Bettina was so insistent, and she agreed we could bring a dessert. I hope you don't mind."

Megan smiled. "Why would I mind? You know I like Bettina, and I'd love to finally meet her family after all these years the two of you have worked together. Meanwhile, I'll plan something really rich and decadent to contribute to the event."

As the two of them returned to their task, Megan sensed the time was right to broach the topic that hung between them.

"Mom," she said, still slicing, "we need to talk."

Laura didn't answer.

"About . . . my future. Seriously, Mom, I need to plan beyond returning to school after Thanksgiving and finishing the semester. That part's a given, but I haven't a clue what to do beyond that."

This time when Laura looked up, tears teased her pale blue eyes, and Megan's heart constricted. The last thing in the world she wanted to do was to cause her mother pain, but putting off this conversation any longer was not going to make the problem disappear.

She was about to point out that fact when Laura set down her knife and said, "You're right. I know you are. And I agree that we need to discuss this. But can we wait until after dinner? Please, Megan. I just need a little more time to gather my thoughts."

Megan nodded. "Sure, Mom. Of course we can."

She finished slicing the mushrooms and scraped them into the growing pile of freshly cut vegetables in the bowl, wondering if the conversation would really be any easier after they ate than before. But if that's the way her mom wanted it, then that's the way it would be.

* * *

"THAT SALAD WAS PERFECT, MOM. Did you enjoy it?"

Laura studied Megan's face, even as she tried to concentrate on her words. The salad? Yes, it was very good . . . wasn't it? She hadn't really noticed. "Excellent," she said, forcing a smile. "I'm glad you suggested something light. After lasagna for lunch, I really wasn't hungry for much else."

"Neither was I."

Laura watched as Megan folded and refolded her napkin. It was only a matter of time until she broached the subject again. Laura knew she couldn't put her off any longer.

"Mom, about my plans . . . "

Laura reached across the table and laid her hand on Megan's. The girl immediately stopped fiddling with her napkin and looked up into her mother's eyes. "We have to talk about this, Mom."

Laura nodded, taking a deep breath in an effort to calm the jitters in her stomach. "Of course we do."

Tears popped into Megan's eyes then, and Laura's heart twisted. How could she be so selfish? Her daughter was hurting. No doubt she had believed she and Alex were a forever item, or she would never have compromised her beliefs and gotten involved with him sexually. Laura knew that as certainly as she knew her own name.

"Just so you know," Megan said, the first tear rolling from her eye onto her cheek, "there's absolutely no chance for Alex and me to get back together. I want to be clear on that before we go any farther in this discussion." She shook her head, and her unruly locks bounced on her shoulders. "I thought we were in love, Mom. He said he loved me, and I was so sure I loved him, though I realize now how foolish that was. But I trusted him. I was . . . wrong. About everything."

Laura nodded and scooted her chair closer so she could pull her child into her arms. "I know," she said, caressing Megan's back. "I know this wasn't something that happened lightly. And I'm so sorry you were hurt by it."

Megan's shoulders shook then, and the sobs began to pour out. Laura pulled her closer and let her own tears fall.

Help me, Lord, she prayed silently. *Show me what to say, what to do. Get us through this, Father, please!*

Though the only sound she heard in response was her daughter's continued cries, she knew they weren't alone, and she took comfort in that.

Chapter 8

Jenny's arthritis was acting up that morning. She imagined it had something to do with the storm that was blowing in, and she was more than a little tempted to leave the shop closed and stay home that Tuesday. But she knew the clinic would be open, and that meant Dr. Laura Branson would be at work, caring for as many patients as necessary. That also meant that Laura might very well follow through on her promise to return to the shop at noon, and Jenny wasn't about to chance having her show up and find the Closed sign up and the door locked.

No, there was more to Laura's visits than a passing curiosity to learn more than she already knew about Elizabeth Blackwell. Jenny had been spending time in prayer for Laura, and she was now more convinced than ever that it was no accident that Laura had popped into the shop the previous week and the two women were now meeting regularly.

"I don't really have a choice then, do I, Lord?" she said, pulling her warmest coat from the entryway closet and stuffing her arms into the sleeves. "If this is Your divine appointment, I dare not miss it. Just please give me ears to hear when You direct me in this matter—and a heart to respond. You know my greatest desire is to be used by You, Father, however You wish . . . and for as long as You wish."

She smiled as she buttoned her coat. "I must admit that I do get weary some days. You've blessed me so much, Lord, so I'm not complaining. But I will say that there are times when I get really anxious to come home."

Jenny slung her purse over her shoulder and picked up her gloves and car keys. "But it doesn't look like that's going to happen today—at least not right at the moment. So for now, I'm off to open my shop and wait for Laura's lunchtime visit. And You know, Lord, if You want to send a customer or two my way before Laura arrives, I surely would appreciate that."

Sufficiently bundled to face the blustery weather, she stepped outside and pulled the door shut behind her, heading for her car in the detached garage.

* * *

ALEX BLEW INTO HIS CLASPED HANDS, trying to keep warm as he joined the throngs moving from class to class. He'd been late to his first one, and he knew he needed to pull things together before his academic standings dropped so low that his father would follow through on his threat to stop funding his education. The last thing Alex wanted was more student loan debt hanging over his head, but his only other option would be to drop out of school, get some dead-end job, and start paying his own way through life. No way was he about to do that, so he was going to have to get serious about his studies.

It'd be a lot easier if Megan would call, he fumed silently, picking up the pace as he zeroed in on the doorway that would lead down the hall to his next class. *It makes it even harder to study when all I can do is think about her and wonder what she's doing. Why is she ignoring me? What's going on with her that she doesn't at least respond to my messages? You'd think she'd care about my feelings.* The thought that she might have met someone else flitted into his mind, but he shoved it away.

He reached his destination and yanked the door open, only to get pushed aside by three male students barreling outside amidst laughter and conversation so intense they didn't even notice him. Irritated, he waited until they passed and then stepped inside, welcoming the blast of warm air. He unbuttoned his jacket as he hurried down the hallway, confident now that he would at least get into the room and sit down before class started. This particular professor was not one to ignore tardiness and even seemed to take some sort of diabolical pleasure in humiliating any latecomers. Alex had been on the receiving end of the man's pointed comments before, and he wasn't about to be again today.

Hoping to enter unnoticed, he quietly walked into the room and breathed a sigh of relief as he slid into a seat. He'd made it. Now if he could just concentrate enough to get through this class and the next, it would be time to break for lunch. He'd already decided that before he got anything to eat he was going to try once more to reach Megan on her cell phone. If she didn't answer or call back this time, he'd give up until after the Thanksgiving holidays since he was going home to visit his folks for the long weekend. Surely when it was over he'd return to school to find out that Megan had also come back. At least then she could no longer avoid or ignore him. Sooner or later, he was going to confront her— and somehow win her back.

❋ ❋ ❋

LAURA WAS STILL FEELING RAW from the aftereffects of the tears she'd shared with Megan the night before, so it didn't take much to get her emotions going again. The last patient had stolen Laura's heart from the moment his mother carried him into the office. The three-year-old's thumb was stuffed in his mouth and his face nearly buried in his mom's shoulder, but his wide, dark eyes had peeked out at her, questioning and challenging—and frightened.

It had taken the better part of the fifteen-minute consultation and exam to connect with him, but by the time Laura had written out a prescription to treat his bronchitis, the boy was grinning at her as if they'd known one another forever.

I love my patients, she thought, snagging her coat and purse from the hook on the wall beside her desk. *Some more than others, simply because they're easier to get along with. But the kids?* She smiled. *They're my favorites. I just wish they were all as easily treatable as this one.* The fragment of a thought skittered through her mind, teasing her with the realization that she would soon have a grandchild, but she pushed past it. She opened the door and nearly collided with Bettina, who appeared to have been about to enter Laura's office. They exchanged surprised glances and then laughed.

"We've got to stop meeting this way," Laura quipped.

"That's for sure," Bettina said, stepping back a bit. "I just wanted to let you know there's a lull in the waiting room if you want to take a break or something."

Laura nodded. "Exactly what I was thinking. In fact, I'm headed out for a quick lunch and visit with a friend. I should be back in an hour or so."

Bettina raised her eyebrows. "Again? Well, now, this is getting to be a habit—taking real lunch breaks like a regular person." She shook her head. "Never thought I'd see it. Must be a real special friend."

Laura smiled, knowing Bettina was fishing. "She is," she said and left it at that, heading for the doorway. She wanted to have time to pick up some hot soup to take along for lunch. That was the agreement she'd insisted on with Jenny before leaving the day before. Jenny would provide the tea and the stories, while Laura supplied the lunch. She doubted the soup would compare to lasagna, but it would just have to do.

She was relieved to see the snow was still holding off, though the temperature continued to drop and the wind howled and swirled around her, nearly blowing her through the door of Jenny's Treasures as she carried her purse in one hand and the bag with the containers of hot vegetable soup in the other.

"You came!" Jenny's voice sounded as delighted as her expression appeared, warming Laura's heart. Though she sensed she had much to learn from Jenny's stories about Dr. Elizabeth Blackwell, she also knew that a great part of her attraction to their daily meetings was time spent with the elderly lady.

"Did you have your doubts?" Laura asked, smiling as she followed her friend into the back room.

"Not really," Jenny admitted, already reaching for the teapot that sat waiting on the single-burner hot plate. "But I must admit, I wondered if this turn in the weather might give you second thoughts about coming."

Laura shook her head. "Not at all. In fact, I brought us some hot soup. I figured that would be perfect on a day like this."

"Absolutely," Jenny agreed, pouring their tea before settling down on the couch.

Laura was already busying herself getting the lids off their individual containers and retrieving napkins and plastic spoons from the bag. In moments they had offered thanks for their meal and were enjoying the soup and tea.

"Now," Jenny said, setting down her spoon and turning to Laura. "Where were we when we left off yesterday?"

"Elizabeth had just announced to her older sisters that she didn't know what she would be when she grew up, but she knew it would be something hard."

Jenny's eyes shone, and she nodded. "And she was quite right, wasn't she? Despite the fact that there ended up being nine siblings in all, it seemed Little Shy was always grouped with those two older sisters, sort of the 'odd man out,' or fifth wheel, I suppose. Not only did the brother born before Elizabeth die, but the one born soon after her died as well. But frail, tenacious little Elizabeth continued to thrive."

"It's as if God designed her personality for the very challenges that lay ahead of her," Laura observed.

"Exactly. And though her mother gave birth thirteen times in all, two more siblings died as infants. It seemed all the children except Elizabeth were paired together, while she was the only one without a partner close to her age. She loved all her siblings, and they loved her, but her birth order seemed to reinforce her standing as a loner, something that continued throughout much of her life."

"I had forgotten that Dr. Blackwell came from such a large family." Laura paused, nearly mentioning her own situation but reconsidering when she realized she didn't want to discuss Peter. Jenny knew of Laura's losses, but to her credit she seemed to respect Laura's unspoken desire to avoid the subject.

"She certainly did," Jenny said. "And as I mentioned, the siblings were close. The entire family was, for that matter. But it was Elizabeth's father who was her favorite. And though he didn't admit it aloud, everyone knew Little Shy was his favorite as well."

Jenny took another spoonful of soup before continuing. "You know, his influence on Elizabeth was quite strong. Mr. Blackwell believed wholeheartedly that all his children—boys *and* girls—should have every opportunity for a well-rounded education. Elizabeth took to that like the proverbial duck to water. He instilled in them the belief that they could do or be anything they set their mind to, and for the most part, they all responded."

Jenny picked up a napkin and dabbed at her mouth. "They were a faith-filled family, you know, having daily prayer and Bible study in their home, as well as attending church regularly. The biggest event on their social calendar was missionary week in May. The entire clan would sit, enthralled, as they listened to stories of faraway lands and exotic adventures. These stories only served to fuel the family's passion for social change, including educational reforms and full rights for women. But one of Mr. Blackwell's greatest passions was to see slavery overthrown."

Laura had just taken a sip of tea. She set the cup down and eyed Jenny with surprise. "Now that's something I didn't know."

"Many people don't," Jenny said. "And Elizabeth picked up her father's anti-slavery torch and carried it throughout her lifetime, especially after relocating to America and eventually finding herself embroiled in the Civil War." She leaned forward. "One of the most interesting points of all is that the Blackwell family came from Bristol, a major slave-trading port in England until slavery was outlawed there in 1807. Sadly, many of Samuel Blackwell's colleagues continued to smuggle slaves to the colonies, which enraged Samuel. He had his own issues to deal with about that, though. Despite the man's personal feelings against slavery, he supported his family through his sugar refinery business, an industry almost completely dependent on slave labor in the colonies where sugar cane was raised and harvested."

"That must have been difficult for the entire family."

"I'm sure it was. It was a hypocrisy that Samuel wrestled with for many years, even as he continued to speak out against slavery. And not without repercussion, I might add. Those with antislavery views weren't actively persecuted in England, but they were known as Dissenters and were considered second-class citizens. They were barred from certain professions, and their children were not allowed to attend many of the better schools. For that reason the Blackwells kept their children at home and educated them there."

"Homeschoolers."

Jenny nodded. "Exactly."

Laura glanced at her watch. "I hate to do this, but I'd better get back. I'm still a working woman, you know."

"You certainly are." Jenny chuckled. "And I understand completely."

She rose from the couch, and Laura did the same.

"The soup was delicious," Jenny said. "And the company was even better."

"I feel the exact same way." Laura hesitated. "Would you mind if I come back tomorrow?"

"Mind? My dear, I'm looking forward to it already."

Laura picked up her coat and purse and turned to go, then paused. She glanced back at Jenny, wondering if she should give voice to the thought that had popped into her mind.

"Do you . . . " she took a quick breath, "do you have plans for Thanksgiving?"

Jenny appeared surprised. "Thanksgiving? Why, that's this Thursday, isn't it?" She smiled. "I imagine I'll spend the day at home. No sense opening the shop on a holiday. No one would come in—not even you."

"You can't do that. Stay home alone, I mean. Please, will you join us? Megan and me? We're having dinner with Bettina and her family—the receptionist at the clinic. You met her once, remember? It would be lovely to have you come along."

Jenny blinked. "Have dinner at your friend's home? Oh, I don't think so. It would be such an imposition."

"Not at all," Laura insisted. "Trust me. Bettina says their family's motto is The More, the Merrier. And I believe her. In fact, when I mentioned you might be alone for Thanksgiving, she insisted I bring you. If I show up without you, she'll give me a scolding I'll never forget. So you have to come." She offered her warmest smile. "Besides, you're only one little lady. How much imposition could you possibly be?"

The older woman's face softened. "You might be surprised how much turkey I can eat. It's one of my very favorite foods."

"Well then, Megan and I will plan to pick you up Thursday afternoon, and we'll all head over to Bettina's to see how much damage we can do to her turkey. I'll call before we come."

It was settled. Laura hugged her friend good-bye and headed for the door, already anticipating the upcoming holiday feast.

Chapter 9

MEGAN HAD STAYED in bed longer than usual that morning, indulging what seemed like an ever-growing need for sleep. She'd heard that sometimes happened with pregnant women.

"Pregnant women." She spoke the words aloud, even as she pulled herself out of bed and threw on a robe and slippers. She had come to terms with the fact that she was indeed pregnant, even if only a couple of months along, but pregnant was a condition, while pregnant women seemed more of a definition. She wasn't sure if she was ready to apply that to herself yet.

By the time she got out of the shower and piled her still damp hair up on top of her head with a giant clippie, she was ready to head for the kitchen and have a late breakfast.

She glanced at her watch. Breakfast? It would be more like lunch by now. Wow, she really had stayed in bed a long time!

First things first. Regardless of the time of day, she needed coffee. Just the smell of it dripping into the pot got her blood moving, and she decided to go all out and scramble a couple of eggs. It was one o'clock in the afternoon by the time she sat down to the table with her eggs and toast, and she was more than ready to devour it all by then.

She'd scarcely dug in when she heard her phone ring. She glanced around. Where had she left it? Still in her room, no doubt. Dropping her fork onto the plate, she scurried down the hall and made it just in time to snatch up the phone before the call went to voice mail.

"Hello?" she said, fully expecting to hear her mom's voice on the other end.

"Megan?"

Her thoughts froze, right along with her heart.

Alex. Why hadn't she taken the time to check caller ID before answering?

She swallowed. There was no need to be rude. She would simply refuse to give him any encouragement. Their relationship was over, and that was that. "Hello, Alex."

"Megan, I've been trying to reach you for days. Didn't you get my messages?"

"Yes, I saw that you called."

"So why didn't you call back?"

She hesitated. Did she even want to answer that question? Could she, even if she wanted to?

"I've been . . . busy. Besides, I believe we've already said everything we need to say to each other."

Apparently he chose to ignore her last statement, focusing only on her first reason for not calling. "Busy? Doing what? You're at home, right? At your mom's?"

She nodded. "Um, yeah. I came home a few days ago."

"Why? Is something wrong? Why didn't you just wait for Thanksgiving and go then?"

"I don't know. Just wanted to come home early, I guess."

"So everything's OK?"

She swallowed. Everything was far from OK, but she wasn't about to tell him that. "Sure. Everything's fine." She knew she should at least ask about him, how he was doing, but she just couldn't bring herself to do it. What she really wanted to do was scream at him and ask why he was calling her at all, why he wasn't off with his precious Chloe, making plans for their first Thanksgiving together. But that might indicate she still cared, and she wasn't about to give him that impression, especially after what he'd done to her when she trusted him. She gnawed the inside of her lip and said nothing.

"I'm glad to hear that. I was worried."

Worried? About me? Why do I not believe that? Still, she said nothing.

"Megan? Are you there?"

"I'm . . . here."

"You don't sound OK. Are you sure everything's all right?"

"Everything's fine. I just wanted to come home early and spend some extra time with my mom. That's all."

She heard him sigh. "If you say so. Does that mean you'll be back after Thanksgiving weekend?"

"Of course I will. Why wouldn't I?" She scolded herself for snapping at him, but the longer they talked, the harder it was to restrain her emotions.

"Just asking," he said, a defensive tone in his voice. "I guess I . . . I'm just hoping to see you again. When you get back, I mean. So we can talk."

"Talk?" Megan frowned. "Why would we do that? It's over between us, remember? You ended it with your behavior. What's left to talk about?"

"Megan, please, listen to me." He paused. "I . . . I know I've been a jerk, and I made a big mistake. I really did, and I miss you something terrible. Is there any chance we can . . . try to work things out? Start over again, maybe?"

She caught her breath, laying her free hand on her stomach as she tried to digest his words. Work things out? Start over? Was he kidding?

"I need to go," she said, her voice beginning to shake right along with her knees. "I can't talk anymore, Alex."

"Megan, don't go. Please. Not yet."

"I have to. I . . . I'm busy doing something in the kitchen."

"It can wait."

"No, it can't. I'm sorry, Alex."

"Then call me back. Please. I've got classes this afternoon, but I'm free all evening. Will you call me then, and we can talk? I'll even come there if you want me to."

"No!" The sharpness of her answer seemed to revive her strength, and she drew up straight. "Do not come here, Alex. Not under any conditions. Do you hear me? Do not come here."

"Fine." The hurt was evident in his voice. "I won't. But call me, please. Please, Megan. Say you will."

She swallowed. "I don't know, Alex. I really don't know. Maybe."

She disconnected the call and tossed the phone on her unmade bed, and then turned and headed back to the kitchen. Her eyes swam with tears as she stared at her uneaten breakfast. Why had she answered the phone? Why had she said she might call him when she knew she wouldn't? Why was he complicating everything by saying he wanted her back? And why, oh why, did her heart cry out to at least consider what he was saying? Would it really hurt to talk to him? After all, they were going to have a baby together.

Together? There was a time, not that long ago, when such a thing would have seemed a joyous event, though she would have envisioned it happening after they were married. But at least then she had felt secure in Alex's love. That security was gone now because, quite obviously, he had never really loved her. And even with a baby between them, she questioned that they could ever have any sort of relationship again. To be truthful, she didn't even want to try.

❅ ❅ ❅

THE AFTERNOON HAD BEEN EVEN SLOWER than the morning, and Laura was about ready to call it a day when Bettina rapped on her office door and then pushed it open and stepped inside without waiting for an answer.

"Come on in," Laura said.

"I already did." Bettina smiled. "I knew you didn't have any patients."

Laura nodded. "They cleared out early today, didn't they?"

"I think they're all waiting for Wednesday afternoon. You know how busy it gets right before a holiday. They'll have us all here till midnight."

"You're probably right." Laura sighed. "At least, it sure seems to go that way, doesn't it? If I remember right, that's exactly what happened this time last year."

"Um hmm." Bettina nodded. "I remember that night, for sure. Thought we'd never get out of here. Earl was about fit to be tied." She chuckled. "Complained the whole next day while he was cooking. But once we all sat down to eat and started raving about his food, he never mentioned it again."

Bettina's words sparked a memory in Laura's mind. Jenny. She'd invited Jenny to join them for Thanksgiving dinner, just as Bettina had suggested. But had Bettina thought to alert Earl to the possibility? Was the invitation truly a valid one? Or would Earl end up fit to be tied again?

She took a deep breath. "Um, Bettina." She paused.

The woman planted her hands on her hips. "I'm listening, but you're not talking. I don't read minds, you know."

Laura smiled. "I know. And I'm sorry. It's just that I followed through on your suggestion."

CHAPTER 9   83

Bettina's dark eyebrows shot upward. Still she waited.

"I invited Jenny to join us for dinner at your place on Thursday."

Laura watched as Bettina's eyebrows dropped and her face softened. "That's it? You're all worked up because you invited your friend to come and eat with us?" She laughed and shook her head. "I sure would hate to see you how you act when you *really* do something dangerous. Besides, didn't I tell you to invite her?"

"You did, yes." Laura paused, relieved by Bettina's reaction. "But shouldn't we have asked Earl's permission first? After all, he's the one doing all the cooking." She frowned as a thought popped into her mind. "Bettina, he does know Megan and I are coming, right?"

Bettina shook her head. "Honestly, you'd think this was a big deal or something. Yes, Earl knows you're coming, and he's just fine with that. The more, the merrier, remember? And besides, since when does a person need permission to invite someone to come and eat with them? Seems to me the Bible's full of verses about feeding the hungry and sharing our blessings." She smiled down at Laura. "I'm just glad you followed through and invited your friend, and I guarantee Earl will be too. There's nothing that man likes better than people coming over to *ooh* and *aah* over his cooking. And Thanksgiving is his favorite day of the year. He's already started working on some of his specialties, things that take a few days to prepare. So bring Jenny and Megan with you, and come on over any time you're ready."

Laura's heart warmed. Bettina was indeed a dear friend, and now that she was assured she'd done the right thing by inviting Jenny, she was once again looking forward to the gathering on Thursday.

"By the way," she said, pulling herself back to the present. "You didn't come in here to talk to me about

Thursday, did you? I'm afraid I got you off track. Was there something else you wanted to discuss?"

"Only that I wanted to go ahead and go home a few minutes early. The waiting room was empty last time I looked, and I'd sure like to get home as soon as possible this evening. Earl Jr., just got home from college a couple hours ago, and I can't wait to see him."

Home from college. The words penetrated a nerve, and Laura flinched. Hiding her reaction, she smiled. "Absolutely. Get going, Bettina—while the getting's good. You know if you hang around, some last-minute straggler will come in and then you'll never escape."

"That's the truth," Bettina agreed, turning toward the door. "Besides, like I said, you know we'll be getting out of here late on Wednesday, so we might as well take advantage now." She turned back and offered a last smile at Laura. "Dr. Farmington left an hour or so ago, so the place is pretty empty now. You'd better get going too. You sure you don't want me to wait until you leave?"

"Not at all," Laura insisted. "You go on. I'll be right behind you, I promise."

Laura watched Bettina close the door behind her. After a moment she turned back to her desk to finish writing out her last report. Then she would keep her promise to Bettina and head for home.

✳ ✳ ✳

MEGAN'S FINGER NEARLY TWITCHED at the temptation to punch in the familiar speed dial number that would connect her with Alex. She'd done her best throughout the day to ignore his plea to call him that evening, but her resolve was wearing down.

What is wrong with me? The thought pounded through her mind, over and over again, as she tried to argue it down. *Why would I even consider calling him back after the way he treated me? What kind of a person am I? And why does he want me back now? What about his new girlfriend? Besides, what makes me think he wouldn't treat me exactly the same way as he did before if I gave him another chance?*

She tried to tell herself it was curiosity, that she just wanted to hear what he had to say, and then she'd remind him in no uncertain terms that they were through, period, and never to call her again. But how realistic was that? Sooner or later she'd have to tell him about the baby, wouldn't she? Even if she didn't, Alex was no dummy. Eventually he would learn about her condition, and simple math would tell him it was his child. Then what? What if he wanted to be involved in his baby's life? What if he went so far as to fight her for custody? Was that possible? Could he do that? And then there was the issue of financial support. He should do his part, but did she even want him to?

Megan sighed and plunked back down at the kitchen table, where she'd nursed a tepid cup of cocoa for the last fifteen minutes, taking a sip and then jumping up and pacing before returning to her spot. So far today she'd accomplished absolutely nothing, and things weren't looking anymore promising as evening approached.

She knew they were expecting snow sometime tonight, and she told herself she'd done the right thing by coming home a few days early. At least she wouldn't be driving in the middle of a storm the next day. But what good had it done? She and her mom still hadn't had any deep discussions about her future. Despite the good cry she'd had in her mother's arms the night before, Megan had yet to make even one decision about what to do beyond returning to school and completing the current semester. What was she to do after that?

And there was the thing with Alex. At least it had been a lot less confusing when he was out of the picture. Now he wanted back in. Should she consider it, for the child's sake? Was it possible that one night's behavior didn't really reflect his true character? After all, it wasn't as if she didn't bear at least some of the guilt.

She glanced at the phone, on the table next to her cocoa mug. How many times had she picked it up, ready to call, only to put it down again? Maybe she should call and get it over with. It was obvious she wasn't going to be able to let go of the problem by ignoring it.

Picking up the phone, she stared as if expecting it to light up with a message that would tell her what to do. Before she could make a decision, she heard keys in the front door and her mom's voice calling out, "Megan? I'm home."

Relieved, she dropped the phone back onto the table and hurried to meet her mother in the entryway. She felt as if she'd dodged a bullet, at least for the time being, and maybe now with her mom at home she could forget about calling Alex.

"You're early," she said, greeting Laura with a hug and a peck on the cheek.

Laura smiled as she pulled off her coat and hung it in the entryway closet. "We were slow today, and both Dr. Farmington and Bettina headed for home, so I decided to do the same."

"That's great, but I'm afraid I don't have anything made for dinner yet."

"Not a problem." Laura hooked her arm with Megan's as they returned to the kitchen. "We'll order Chinese. Doesn't that sound good? Fried rice and chow mein, and maybe even some egg drop soup."

Megan was surprised that her taste buds reacted so favorably. She hadn't felt much like eating all day. "Sounds fantastic. Can we get some sweet-and-sour pork too?"

Laura laughed. "I don't see why not. I'll get the number and you can order while I go put on my slippers. My feet are killing me."

The food arrived in under an hour, and Megan ate enough to make up for all she'd missed earlier in the day. Having her mom there for support made resisting Alex so much easier. No wonder she'd come home early! She needed her mother's strength and wisdom during this crucial time in her life.

Megan glanced across the table at her mother, who had laid down her fork and appeared to be through eating.

"Mom?"

Laura raised her head and smiled. "What is it, honey?"

"We need to talk, you know. About the baby."

Laura's smile faded. "I thought we did that. Last night."

Megan shook her head. "No. Not really. I cried, and you comforted me and assured me everything would be all right. But that's not what I mean. We need to talk about the future. What I'm going to do."

A flicker of misgiving crossed Laura's face. "I thought you were going back to school on Monday and finish the semester as planned."

"I am. But then what? Mom, I know the baby isn't due for seven months, but it will only be five months by the time the semester ends. Then what?"

A hint of tears sprang into her mother's eyes, and the color drained from her face, making her appear older than Megan had ever seen her look before. The reminder that she had done this to her mom by her poor choices and lack of good judgment squeezed Megan's heart in a vise grip.

"I'm sorry, Mom," she whispered, reaching over to lay her hand on her mother's arm. "I am so sorry."

Everything in her cried out for her mother to deny that it was as bad as Megan thought, to reassure her yet again that all would be well. But Megan watched as her mother's face crumpled before she buried it in her hands and began to sob. It was as if the scene from the night before had just reversed itself, and now Megan was the one needing to offer comfort.

Quickly she responded and scooted near her mother, wrapping her arms around her and letting her cry on her shoulder. Whatever had she been thinking to put such a burden on her mother? Hadn't the poor woman been through enough, losing her husband and son, working hard to raise her remaining child and to give her everything possible so she could have a good and honorable life?

And how had Megan repaid her? By betraying her and then dumping her problems in her mother's lap, expecting her to fix them like she had when Megan was still a little girl. Well, she wasn't a little girl anymore, and it wasn't right to expect her to come to the rescue, especially now. For once in her life, Megan was going to have to deal with the consequences of her actions without depending on her mother to do it for her.

If that meant at least considering giving Alex another chance, then so be it. Maybe the two of them could work through this baby situation on their own and leave Megan's mother out of it. If not, Megan would simply have to deal with things on her own. It was obvious she had overestimated her mother's strength and stamina. Megan was just glad she realized it before it was too late.

Chapter 10

WEDNESDAY MORNING AT THE CLINIC was slow but steady, with people streaming in and out on a relatively manageable basis. As a result, Laura had opted to keep her daily appointment with Jenny, even buying a couple of ham sandwiches along the way.

Picking her way carefully across the icy sidewalk and up to the shop's front door, she stepped inside, pleased to see that Jenny was alone in the shop. The older woman looked up from the register and caught Laura's eye. Their smiles connected immediately.

"I'm so glad you're here," Jenny said. "How are the streets out there? I didn't have much trouble coming in this morning."

"They're not bad at all. Of course, we're supposed to get a second coating of the white stuff tonight, so who knows what it will be like tomorrow?"

"I was thinking that very thing. Why don't I just drive my own car and meet you at your friend's house tomorrow? There's no sense in your driving all the way over to pick me up. It would save you some time."

Laura smiled. "Time is something I have plenty of tomorrow. Megan is baking today while I'm at work, so we really don't have anything else we have to do before we go to dinner." She shook her head. "No, you don't need to drive. We'll gladly pick you up and take you home later."

"All right. If you're sure." Jenny turned and pulled back the blue curtain, beckoning Laura to join her. "Will you turn over the Open sign and lock the door?"

Laura did and then proceeded to the rear of the store, already anticipating Jenny's hot tea.

"I hope you don't mind that I brought sandwiches today," she said. "I thought about soup again but decided to do something different."

"Sandwiches are fine." Jenny poured tea into their cups. "Soup too. I'll eat most anything that's set in front of me."

"Well, then, I imagine you'll eat plenty tomorrow. From what I understand, Bettina's husband is a serious cook who takes great pleasure in feeding his guests until they beg for mercy."

Jenny laughed. "I'm looking forward to that meal more than you can imagine—and the family time too." A wistful look crossed her face. "It's been a while since I've had any of my own family home for Thanksgiving dinner. You must be thrilled that your daughter is with you for the holidays."

A searing knife jabbed at Laura's heart as she thought of the evening before. She was embarrassed that she had lost her composure in front of her daughter. Laura was the mother, after all, the mature and strong one . . . right?

Right. She had crumpled like a worn-out sheet of tissue paper. Poor Megan had spent the evening playing the role of comforter, and by the time Laura had recovered, they'd agreed to put off their discussion about future plans for yet another day. Of course, that brought them to today, which meant Laura would by no means get home early enough for that discussion to take place tonight. If Bettina was right—and she usually was—the clinic's waiting room would be full to busting by late afternoon, and no one would be going home until well into the night.

She sighed, remembering Jenny's comment. "Yes," Laura agreed, "I'm really happy to have Megan home with me right now."

Jenny nodded and smiled, and then bowed her head to offer a brief prayer of thanksgiving. Laura joined her, and then unwrapped her sandwich. She wasn't really hungry, but she imagined she should eat since she no doubt had a very long and busy afternoon and evening ahead of her.

"So," Jenny said after taking a sip of tea and setting her cup back on the saucer, "Megan is baking something to take to dinner tomorrow. What can I bring? I'd like to contribute something too."

Laura raised her eyebrows. She hadn't thought to ask that question, though if she had Bettina would no doubt have said Jenny didn't need to bring anything at all or that she would be welcome to bring anything she'd like.

"I imagine you can bring most anything. There will undoubtedly be more food there than any ten armies could eat, so what's one more salad or dessert?"

"I'm sure you're right. I'll think about it this afternoon and come up with something appropriate, I'm sure."

Laura smiled and took a bite of her sandwich. She waited, knowing Jenny would resume the story of Dr. Elizabeth Blackwell in her own time. Sure enough, about halfway through her lunch, Jenny set her sandwich down and leaned back, picking up the quilt.

"We've talked about Little Shy's birth and early childhood," she said, fingering the square with the Christmas rattle. "Maybe we should move on a bit in her timeline."

Laura agreed. She was anxious to learn more about how this amazing woman had been drawn into medicine, a profession that strictly barred the female gender at that point in history.

Jenny indicated a bright, reddish orange patch in the quilt that resembled leaping flames. "This represents a turning point in the lives of the entire Blackwell family—not to mention many others in Bristol at the time. It was late October 1831. Though the Blackwells lived comfortably, thanks to Samuel's sugar refinery business, there were more than six-hundred paupers living in Bristol's poorhouse. Thousands of destitute parents sold their children, some as young as five or six, into work gangs, where they labored in deplorable conditions and seldom had enough food to sustain them."

When Jenny paused, Laura found herself feeling guilty about eating her sandwich. She knew it was silly, but she placed what was left on her plate and waited for Jenny to continue.

"Not only England but the entire continent of Europe was sinking into economic depression. It was inevitable that revolution would follow. Before October was over, Bristol was on fire. Rioters burned down the jail and released all the prisoners. They burned everything in their path—until they came to the Anglican church, where Samuel Blackwell took a stand. History isn't clear about what Samuel said or did, but the church still stands to this day, and Little Shy's father came out of the riots with the reputation of a hero."

"And the family business?"

"The refinery survived the fire, but Samuel saw the writing on the wall. His future prospects were not good, not with the city, and even the nation and continent, in turmoil. And then things went from bad to worse."

Laura leaned forward. How much worse could the situation be?

"The cholera epidemic that had been sweeping across Europe arrived in Bristol. It was time, Samuel Blackwell decided, to head for the Promised Land—America. And so, in August 1832, the entire family set sail for the United States."

Laura felt her eyes grow wide. She knew Elizabeth Blackwell had been born in England and had eventually become the first woman doctor in America. She also knew

Elizabeth had surmounted incredible obstacles to make that happen. But it had never occurred to her that historical events had played such a huge part in orchestrating the outcome. And why did she continually feel as if she should be taking away personal applications to her own life each time she heard another installment of Dr. Blackwell's story?

※ ※ ※

ALEX WATCHED THE CLOCK ON THE WALL above his professor's head, wondering if it would ever move. It seemed like he'd been in this same class for hours. Would it never end? Once he got out of here he could throw some things in his duffel bag and hit the road for home. The weather was awful, but he'd made the drive countless times and figured he could probably do it in his sleep.

A movement from across the room caught his eye, and he realized Chloe was trying to get his attention by offering a tentative wave and a smile. He forced himself to smile back, though he didn't want to encourage her. She'd been bugging him all week about letting her come home with him for Thanksgiving so she could meet his parents, but that was the last thing in the world Alex wanted. All it would do was encourage Chloe that their relationship was more serious than it was, and he sure didn't need that. He had to admit, though, that he wouldn't have minded bringing Megan home with him. She'd met his parents once, and they all seemed to hit it off. But then, why wouldn't they? They were all into their faith thing, much more than he was. Admittedly he didn't have that issue to contend with when it came to Chloe.

He averted his eyes from her longing gaze and tried once again to concentrate on the monotone lecture that proceeded from the front of the room. He'd just about succeeded when he felt his phone buzz in his pocket. As unobtrusively as possible, he retrieved the phone and checked the name on the screen.

Megan. At last! His heart raced, as he considered jumping up from his seat and racing out of the room to catch her call before she hung up. He knew he wouldn't make it, though, so he sat tight, clenching his jaws in an effort to squelch his excitement and impatience. The minute he got out of there he was going to listen to her message and call her right back. Chloe wouldn't even rate a "Happy Thanksgiving" in the process.

❄ ❄ ❄

MEGAN SHOULD HAVE REALIZED Alex would still be in class when she called. She very nearly didn't leave a message at all, but decided it was better to say something than hang up. So she'd left a generic sentence or two about talking with him later and hoping he had a nice Thanksgiving with his family. *How is it possible to leave such a meaningless message on his phone when his very existence has completely changed my life?*

As she worked on her seven-layer chocolate and marshmallow cream dessert for the next day, she wondered if she'd made a terrible mistake by calling at all. But the memory of her mother's tears the night before convinced her she'd had no choice.

Mom isn't as strong as I thought she was. She's always been there for me, especially since Dad and Peter died. She was everything—my strength, my counselor, my protector. I know God's the only One who can really fill all those roles, but as a child I needed at least one parent I could count on. And she never let me down.

The thought that she had done so this time flitted through her mind, but she shoved it away. Her mother hadn't let her down; she'd simply allowed Megan to see her for the fallible human being she was. The realization shook Megan, but it also fueled her resolve to take more responsibility for herself and dump less on her already overburdened mother.

Her cell phone rang, jarring her from her baking and her thoughts.

Alex. It had to be.

She rinsed her hands and grabbed a dishtowel to dry them before retrieving her phone from the counter.

Pausing only a moment to confirm it was Alex, she punched the receive button and did her best to quell her nerves as she answered.

"Hello?"

"Megan." He sounded breathless. "I just got out of class, and I'm on my way back to pick up my stuff before I head home. I'm so glad you called. Is everything . . . OK?"

She raised her eyebrows. What did he mean by that? OK in what way? Was she feeling all right? Was everything going well at home? Or was there a deeper meaning? Was he asking if things were OK between them? Surely not. She wasn't about to go there . . . not even close.

"I'm . . . fine," she said, relieved that her voice wasn't trembling. "And you?"

"I'm good." His voice dropped a notch and took on a husky tone. "I'd be a lot better if you were here with me."

Megan opened her mouth to answer, but decided against it.

"Did you hear me?"

"I heard you. I chose not to answer."

He sighed. "Got it. I'm pushing too hard too fast, aren't I? OK, I'll back off. But at least you called me. That's a good sign."

"I . . . " she hesitated, "I'm not sure it's a sign of any kind, Alex. I just called because you asked me to."

"I'm glad you did." She could nearly hear the smile in his voice. "So what are you doing?"

"I'm baking a dessert for tomorrow. Mom and I are going to someone else's house for Thanksgiving dinner."

"I wish you were coming to my house with me. My parents would love to see you again."

Megan shut her eyes and remembered the one visit she'd had with the Williams family. It had been enjoyable, and she'd been pleasantly surprised at the strength of his parents' faith, particularly in light of the fact that Alex seemed not to share it. She had somehow gained hope from that visit that Alex would indeed come back to his Christian roots soon, which in turn helped her rationalize their otherwise questionable relationship.

"Please give them my best, will you? They're very nice people."

"I will. But I still wish you were coming with me. It's going to be a long, lonely weekend without you."

Megan's eye snapped open and she frowned. Talk about pushing too hard too fast! Had he forgotten why their relationship ended, and how quickly he had filled his "long, lonely weekends" with someone else? She longed to ask him those questions, as well as why he wasn't spending the holiday with Chloe, but she managed to hold her words inside. Reminding herself that she needed to take the pressure off her mom and deal with issues on her own, she took a deep breath before answering.

"I . . . I need to get back to work on my dessert. I really do hope you have a good weekend, Alex. Maybe we can talk when we both get back to school next week."

Once again she heard him smiling through his words. "That would be great, Megan. I'll be counting the days."

She said good-bye and ended the connection, laying a hand on her stomach as she tried to focus on the one topic she and Alex needed to discuss. She didn't look forward to broaching the subject with him and certainly hadn't planned to do so anywhere near this soon, but if she really was going to start behaving like a mature woman she'd have to find the strength to open the conversation with him sooner rather than later.

Meanwhile, she had work to do. It would no doubt be several hours before her mom could break away from the clinic and come home, so Megan determined to keep herself busy until then. If that meant whipping up two or three more desserts after this one, so be it. She wasn't about to let herself dwell on the situation with Alex and the baby. There would be enough time for that next week.

Chapter 11

ALEX HAD HOPED THE WORST OF THE STORM would hold off until he made the one hundred-plus-mile drive to his parents' house in Pueblo. Instead he found himself practically crawling down I-25, pelted by high winds and icy snowflakes that coated his windshield faster than his wipers could scrape them off. And if he'd been under any delusion that he was getting out ahead of the traffic, he knew better now. Almost from the start of his trip he'd found himself boxed in by what seemed to be millions of other travelers heading out for the four-day holiday. What would normally be a two-hour drive would no doubt last more than twice that long.

He groaned as he thought of how his mom had asked him not to come until the weather cleared up. "It's supposed to be better by tomorrow. Why don't you just wait and come then?" But, as usual, he had ignored her advice and followed through with his plans to leave the minute he got out of his last class.

I barely took the time to call Megan, he thought, smiling at the memory. She hadn't been overly encouraging, but at least she hadn't shut him down completely. He just wished she'd invited him to stop by her mom's place on the way home. He had to go right by there, after all. And who knows? Maybe she would have broken down and asked him to stay for the holiday instead of going home. His parents would have been disappointed, but he could always blame the weather for his change of plans.

The weather. It sure wasn't getting any better. He shouldn't have used the money his dad sent him for tire chains to take Chloe out to dinner instead. True, she'd been impressed, and it had gone a long way toward getting him what he wanted from her, though he had no doubt he would have gotten it anyway. She had been so much easier than Megan.

Megan. Why had he let things get so out of hand that he'd actually lost a classy girl like her and ended up with someone like Chloe? Sure, Chloe was a looker—every bit as good or better than Megan—but that was about it. As far as Alex could see, she really didn't have anything else going for her. For the life of him he couldn't imagine how she'd ever gotten into medical school—but then, he was there and few people ever thought he would be, so maybe that explained it. Still, Chloe hadn't been much of a challenge, and that was something Alex really enjoyed.

He grinned. No doubt he was in for another challenge now with Megan—winning her back and getting their relationship going again. But he was sure he could do it. If he could just get her alone for a little while—

A thump to the passenger side of his SUV sent the vehicle into a spin, as Alex felt himself thrown against the steering wheel. For a split second he realized he'd been hit by a skidding car and the thought popped through his mind that he should have heeded his mother's continuous warning to wear his seatbelt. Then his vehicle collided with a flash of red to his right, which he fleetingly recognized as a large truck. It was his last conscious thought before his head rocked forward, exploding the windshield as he succumbed to the darkness.

* * *

LAURA WAS EXHAUSTED. Bettina had been right about the last-minute crowd showing up in the clinic's waiting room on Wednesday. Though the morning had been manageable, from the time Laura returned from her lunch with Jenny, everything had changed. Not only had the snow started up again, heavier than the night before, but patients poured through the front door with everything from sneezes and sniffles to sprained ankles and spiking fevers. Apparently they wanted everything fixed in time for Thanksgiving the next day. The two doctors plowed through without a break, while Bettina did her best to keep the waiting room quiet and orderly, even as she filled out paperwork, answered phones, and escorted people to the back offices when their names came up on the list.

Thank goodness that was the last one, Laura thought, practically falling into the chair in her office. She still had some reports to write, and then she was heading home to soak in a hot bath. She was glad she'd thought to warn Megan that she'd probably be late because she sure hadn't had a chance to call her and check in.

Laura glanced at her watch. Nearly eight o'clock! She'd known it was past their usual closing time, but she'd had no idea how late it really was. Maybe she'd better call Megan just in case.

"Everything OK there?" she asked when her daughter answered the phone.

"Sure. Fine, Mom. What about you? You sound tired."

"Exhausted. But I'm almost ready to leave. Just have a few papers to fill out."

"Good. I made some chicken soup. It's simmering on the stove, so you can eat it whenever you get here."

Laura smiled. "That was thoughtful of you. I appreciate it. Did you get your dessert made too?"

Megan chuckled. "Actually, I made three of them. The seven-layer one I told you about, plus an apple pie and some ambrosia. I had to go to the store to get some of the ingredients, but it kept me busy all day."

Laura frowned. "You went out in this awful weather in that little beater car of yours? I'm surprised you were able to stay on the road. Everyone who came in today complained about how awful it was out there."

"They're right—even though my car is *not* a beater. But the wind really is vicious, and the roads are going to ice over bad tonight. I'm glad you're almost ready to come home. You'd better be careful, Mom."

"You know I will be. Besides, that's why I have a *real* car—one with four-wheel drive and snow tires."

"Still, there are a lot of crazy drivers out there." Laura could hear the concern in her daughter's voice. "I'll feel a lot better once you're here, safe and sound."

"It won't be long, I promise." Laura shook her head. "I can't believe you made three desserts. What gave you the idea to do all that?"

Megan paused before answering. "Oh, nothing in particular. I was just in the mood to cook, I guess."

"Well, I'm sure we'll all benefit from the results. Of course, from the sound of things, Bettina's husband has been cooking for days, so between everything the two of you have put together, we probably won't even make a dent."

Megan laughed. "Mom, that's one of the best things about Thanksgiving, remember? Leftovers."

Laura smiled again and clicked off. The sooner she could get those reports filled out and head home, the better.

❊ ❊ ❊

THE STORM HAD SUBSIDED OVERNIGHT and most of the streets were plowed by the time Megan and Laura exited through the kitchen door into the garage, where Laura had parked when she got home the night before. In good weather she often left her car in the driveway overnight, but the blast of winter that had invaded them over the past couple days hardly qualified as good weather.

"Want me to drive?" Megan asked as she opened the trunk and helped her mother set the large flat box with its three desserts inside.

Laura hesitated as she glanced at her daughter. Her first inclination was to say no, but the streets had been cleared, and Megan really was a responsible driver. Besides, they'd be riding in Laura's dependable car rather than Megan's over-grown roller skate.

"Sure. Why not?"

They climbed inside and Megan hit the garage door opener. "So where does your friend live anyway?" She glanced over her shoulder as she backed out into the driveway.

"Just head for Main Street, and I'll direct you from there. She's not far from her shop."

It was only slightly after noon as they made their way the few miles from Laura's house to Jenny's. Traffic was light and the roads were fine. Laura breathed a sigh of relief. She'd caught the weather report early that morning and heard that no more snow was predicted, at least not for several days. She hoped it would hold off long enough for Megan to get back to school on Monday.

We still haven't talked about what she's going to do about the baby, she thought, nearly stumbling over the word, even in her mind. *Baby.* How many times had she stressed the importance of using that word to describe the growing child within the womb? How many times had she cautioned against dehumanizing the little one by refusing to acknowledge that it was indeed a baby? Why then did she have such a difficult time with the word now—now that it applied to her own daughter's very real-life situation?

"Where to now, Mom?"

Laura blinked as she looked out the window, getting her bearings. She hadn't realized they were already turning onto Main Street and were nearing Jenny's home.

"Just a couple more blocks. Then turn left on Elm. I've never actually been there, but she said it's the second house on the right, the one with a white picket fence all the way around."

Within moments they were parked in front of the neat, cozy home, and Laura went to the front door to escort Jenny to the car while Megan kept the engine running. Laura wasn't surprised when her friend came out of the front door carrying a covered dish, which she took from her and carried with one hand while holding Jenny's arm with the other.

"Careful," she cautioned. "The streets are clear, but most of the sidewalks are still slippery." She glanced at the bundled up woman who kept her eyes fixed on the walkway in front of her as she gingerly picked her way across it. "That was sweet of you to bring something, though you certainly didn't need to."

Jenny didn't look up, but Laura could hear the smile in her voice. "I know I didn't need to, but I love to cook and I so seldom get the chance. I made a green bean casserole. It will only take a few minutes to reheat it in the microwave."

"Sounds delicious," Laura said, opening the back door of the car and holding it while Jenny climbed in. Then she went around to the other side and placed the casserole on the floor behind the driver's seat, smiling as she listened to Jenny and Megan greet one another and begin to chat.

Back in her spot in the front passenger seat, she gave Megan directions to Bettina's house, and then settled back as they drove off. Though still a bit apprehensive about invading Bettina's family and home for Thanksgiving dinner, she had to admit that she was also looking forward to the day, whatever it might bring.

Chapter 12

MEGAN ENJOYED DRIVING AND WAS PLEASED that her mom had shown enough confidence in her not to refuse her offer. It hadn't been long ago that Megan knew her mother would have done just that, so she was encouraged. Maybe she was making a few strides toward adulthood and independence after all. And now, with a baby coming, it was none too soon.

She glanced at her mom's animated face as she and Jenny chatted. It was obvious their renewed friendship was blooming, despite the difference in their ages. Megan couldn't see Jenny's face from where she sat, but she'd watched her walk to the car, and it was obvious she had to at least be in her late sixties, possibly even her early seventies.

She's obviously still sharp as a whip, though. Mom's mentioned several times how much she's learning about the life of Elizabeth Blackwell during their times together. You'd think Mom, being a woman doctor, would already know everything possible about the woman. I've certainly heard of her since I've been in med school. So what does this lady know about the doctor that I don't?

She took advantage of the next lull in the conversation and said, "Mrs. Townsend, Mom tells me you know quite a bit about Dr. Blackwell. I've heard of her, but I imagine there's a lot more to her than I realize."

"Indeed," Jenny agreed. "I've been filling your mom in on the young Elizabeth Blackwell—her childhood in Bristol with all eight of her siblings. We left off yesterday just as the Blackwell family was setting sail for America."

"How old was she then?" Megan asked.

"Eleven," Jenny answered. "And a very curious and determined eleven-year-old, I might add. Though the girl started out rather puny and frail and was even referred to by her father as Little Shy, she proved herself to be a lot stronger than anyone would have imagined."

Megan smiled. "I would think she'd have to be when you consider her eventual accomplishments and all she had to do to get there."

"Exactly."

Megan could tell Jenny was warming to the topic.

"If I had my quilt with me I'd show you the patch that represents this particular part of Little Shy's life—a ship on the waves, something Elizabeth didn't especially enjoy, as she spent much of the voyage seasick. It was a trip that would forever change not only the lives of the Blackwell family, but countless others as well."

She chuckled. "Of course, their arrival in the New World was anything but grand. Cholera had struck New York, and many of the streets were deserted. Storefronts were boarded up, and those who remained in their homes had pulled the drapes and drawn the shutters. It was as if the Blackwells had stepped into a ghost town."

Megan raised her eyebrows. It had never occurred to her what it would be like to arrive in a strange land and find it nearly empty. What must the family have thought at that point?

Before she could ask, Jenny continued. "Samuel Blackwell led the way through town with his eight-months pregnant wife, Hannah, at his side, and the nine Blackwell children, along with three aunts, the governess, and the nursemaid, trailing along behind. If any of the New Yorkers took the time to peer out their windows, they must have witnessed quite a procession."

"So what did they do?" Megan asked. "Where did they go? No one met them or took them in when they arrived?"

"No one at all. But they eventually found their way to a hotel near a church, where they paused and offered thanks. Then they obtained lodging and went about settling in to their new surroundings. Samuel quickly connected with some businessmen whose names he had secured before leaving England, and they were instrumental in helping him launch his new sugar manufacturing business. Within two weeks the family had moved into a home of their own. It wasn't nearly as spacious as the one they'd left behind, but at least it was theirs."

Megan was impressed. "That was quick. It sounds like it was a good move for them."

"In many ways it was. But it wasn't without difficulties. Although the family enjoyed exploring their new surroundings and getting 'Americanized,' it was as if many of the problems they thought they'd left behind had instead followed them to their new home."

Before Megan could ask what those problems were, Laura said, "Turn right—here at the stop sign. This is where Bettina's house is."

So, Megan thought, *I guess I won't get to find out the details of the problems Jenny mentioned—unless I can get her to tell us on the way home this evening.*

She smiled at the thought and pulled up in front of the sprawling ranch-style home. Several inches of snow covered the yard, but the walkway to the front door had been shoveled. Three vehicles were already parked in the driveway, and even as Megan stepped out of the car into the street, she saw the front door open. A woman she recognized as her mother's co-worker stepped out onto the porch and waved.

"Come on in," she called. "We've been waiting for you."

Megan smiled at the warm welcome, determined to put her problems behind her for a few hours and enjoy the day.

※ ※ ※

THOUGH LAURA HAD THOUGHT the house appeared spacious as they drove up, it suddenly seemed to shrink as seven adults, twelve children, two dogs, and the most mouth-watering aromas gathered around to welcome the three women. Laura had long known that Bettina had a large family, and had even met Earl and some of the others on occasion, but never all at once.

She did her best to keep everyone's name straight as introductions were made all around, but she imagined she wouldn't do any better at remembering each individual identity than would Megan or Jenny.

Bettina and her sister—whom Laura determined to remember was named Barbara—took the box of desserts and the green bean casserole into the kitchen, while Earl escorted the three women into the living room.

"This is my mama, Ida Mae," he said, beaming at the gray-haired woman sitting in the rocking chair beside the overstuffed sofa. "Mama, this here is the lady that works with Bettina down at the clinic, Dr. Laura Branson. She brought her daughter, Megan, and her friend Mrs. Townsend along with her."

Laura was impressed at Earl's ability to remember names so quickly and accurately, and she was challenged to try harder to do the same.

"You ladies sit down," Earl said. "Bettina and Barbara will be in with some refreshments in just a minute. I need to get back to the kitchen and see to my cooking."

Laura nodded. "Yes, I've heard you're quite the chef. We're all looking forward to your delicious meal."

Earl beamed, widening his shoulders and standing up to what Laura was certain was his full six feet. "Not as much as I'm looking forward to serving it. Now if you'll excuse me."

When he was gone, Laura turned to Ida Mae and smiled. "So you're Earl's mother."

The woman returned her smile and nodded. "I surely am—and proud to be." She shook her head. "That boy has been a joy to me my whole life. Never caused me one ounce of grief." She laughed, the sound joyous but evidencing her age. "Can't say that about my other two. But I love them all the same."

Laura smiled and nodded. She thought she understood . . . but did she? Could she? Her son had died before he ever really had a chance to live. Now Megan was her only offspring. How could she ever compare the two?

"I know exactly what you mean," Jenny said, drawing Laura's attention away from Ida Mae. Jenny sat on the couch to Laura's right, while Megan had parked herself in a recliner across from them.

Jenny was beaming. "I have two grown children, and I love each one of them more than my own life. I wish they lived closer and I could see them more often, but I do know there's nothing either of them could ever do that would change the way I feel about them."

Laura turned back to Ida Mae just in time to see her dark eyes sparkle as she nodded. "Ain't that the truth! It surely is."

This time Laura steered her attention away from both of the older ladies and toward her daughter. Megan was watching her, and as their eyes met, Laura saw a flicker of doubt in the girl's gaze. Her stomach churned. The last thing she wanted to do was to cause her child to doubt her mother's unconditional love. Had she done that? She prayed not, even as she vowed to set aside the time to assure her of that—*before* Megan returned to school on Monday.

"Well, here you all are," Bettina announced as she whisked into the room, carrying a tray of clear mugs filled with fragrant hot cider. Barbara was right behind her, bearing a petitioned snack dish full of offerings that looked too good to name. Laura's taste buds came alive as the drinks and snacks were placed on the coffee table directly in front of the sofa, the spicy aroma of the cider drifting up to tease her nostrils.

"Earl whipped up some bacon-wrapped stuffed mush-rooms," Bettina said, "and he wants your honest opinion, so dive in and let us know what you think."

The sound of a child's giggle interrupted them, and Laura peered beyond Bettina and Barbara at two small boys standing in the doorway. They were the exact same size, dressed alike, and appeared to have come from the same cookie cutter. Laura remembered Bettina mentioning that Barbara had twin grandsons. Quite obviously these were the two, though she couldn't remember if Bettina had ever mentioned their names.

"John and Jacob, you want to come in and visit with these nice ladies?" Barbara asked.

One of the boys nodded, while the other hung back, his wide eyes scanning the group. Laura smiled. She hadn't realized until this moment how very glad she was that she accepted Bettina's invitation. Somehow she sensed there was more to come from this gathering than a nice visit and a good meal, and she was looking forward to finding out what it might be.

❋ ❋ ❋

THE THREE WOMEN had scarcely pulled away from the curb before they started groaning and joking about having to readjust the shock absorbers on the car to handle all the extra weight they were carrying.

"That was, without doubt, one of the best meals I've ever eaten," Megan declared, then quickly cut her eyes to her mother before returning her attention to the road in front of her. "Sorry, Mom. I didn't mean that the way it sounded. You know I think you're one of the best cooks on the planet."

Laura laughed, not at all offended by her daughter's remark. "Don't apologize. Believe me, I feel exactly the same way. Bettina is always telling me what a great cook Earl is, but now we know it for a fact. And as for my own cooking, I hardly do any these days, with you off at college and all. And since you've been home, you've been handling that task quite nicely yourself."

The corner of Megan's mouth turned up in what Laura knew was a pleased smile. "Thanks, Mom. I enjoy doing it."

"That's exactly the way I feel and why I took the opportunity to fix the green bean casserole," Jenny interjected. "When you live alone there's not much sense in putting together a four-course meal. But special occasions bring out the cook in me."

"And you did an excellent job," Laura assured her, glancing back briefly to offer a smile. "I noticed there wasn't any of that casserole left at the end of dinner."

"Surprising, wasn't it? With all the other food on that table, so many delicious dishes to choose from, you'd have thought my casserole would have been lost in the shuffle."

"There really was a huge selection of food, wasn't there?" Megan said. "I think I tried just about everything, and it was all wonderful, even if there were a couple of things I couldn't identify."

Laura's heart rejoiced as she enjoyed the three-way conversation, but also as she reflected on the love and acceptance she'd felt from Bettina's family. Everyone had commented more than once how much Earl Jr. resembled his father, as he actively helped his dad in carving the turkey and serving everyone at the table, reinforcing the welcome Laura had felt since they first stepped through the front door. Even the children had warmed to their guests before the day was over.

And Ida Mae? Laura smiled. What a delightful woman! Her exchange with Jenny about loving all their children equally and that there was nothing any of them could ever do to change that had played in Laura's mind throughout the entire visit.

If I was there for no other reason than to hear that, it was enough. Unconditional love doesn't make the problems go away, but it sure helps keep them in proper perspective.

Once again she glanced over at her daughter, who deftly steered them down the now darkened streets toward Jenny's house. Once again she wondered what would happen to Megan, now that she was pregnant. Would she continue her education and go on to fulfill her—*their*—dream of becoming a doctor? Laura prayed so, though she imagined it would be much more difficult now. And what if Megan chose to abandon the dream altogether? What then?

She shook her head. This had been far too nice a day to mar it now with negative thoughts. She and Megan would sit down together before the weekend was over and do their best to talk their way through to a solution—or at least to a viable plan. Laura just wished she knew what that plan might be.

"Mrs. Townsend," Megan said, "you said earlier that some of the Blackwells' problems seemed to follow them from England to America. What did you mean by that?"

Laura raised her eyebrows. It seemed her daughter was nearly as interested in learning more about Dr. Blackwell as she was. And why not? Megan too was a woman, and she was studying to be a doctor. Elizabeth Blackwell's name was nearly hallowed among female medical students, and yet Laura wondered how many of those students knew the details of this great woman's life.

"I'll be happy to fill in that part of the story for you," Jenny said. "You see, even though things seemed to fall into place for Little Shy and her family, meaning that Samuel got his business off the ground quickly, they found a place to live, and they all enjoyed exploring their new homeland and making friends, there were two primary problems they hadn't been able to leave behind in England."

She paused a moment before continuing. "I suppose you'd classify the first problem as political and social. Your mother and I have already talked about this to some extent, and you may already know that Elizabeth Blackwell was staunchly anti-slavery, both in England and in America. This was a major controversy at the time, with the situation building toward the inevitable Civil War some years later. The Blackwells were quite outspoken about their opposition to slavery, even going so far as to shelter runaway slaves on more than one occasion. But their activism had its repercussions, I'm afraid."

They pulled to a stop at a red light, and the younger women waited for Jenny to continue.

"Samuel Blackwell had always been deeply bothered by the fact that sugar cane was grown by white planters but harvested by black slaves. That the family continued to make their living off the backs of enslaved human beings distressed him, and he actively searched for alternative ways to run his business. It was only natural that as the Blackwell children grew older, their involvement in the abolitionist movement would intensify."

Megan pulled up in front of Jenny's house then. "I can't believe we're here already. I'd really like to hear more of Elizabeth's story."

Laura smiled, pleased at the opportunity that had just popped into her head. "I have an idea. I have to go to the clinic tomorrow, but it shouldn't be nearly as busy as it was on Wednesday. Even if it is, I'll break away for a while in the early afternoon." She directed her attention to Megan. "Why don't the three of us get together for lunch? You're not doing anything in particular tomorrow, are you?"

Megan shook her head. "No, not really."

Laura turned around to face Jenny then. "Will that work for you? We've got all these wonderful leftovers Earl insisted we bring with us. Let's have turkey sandwiches tomorrow, and you can tell us more of Little Shy's story."

"That sounds wonderful," Jenny exclaimed. "The only thing I like better than roasted turkey fresh from the oven is leftover turkey sandwiches. It's a date."

Chapter 13

MEGAN LAY ON HER BACK, staring into the darkness that enveloped the room where she'd slept nearly every night of her growing-up years. Her cell phone perched on the stand beside the bed, red light blinking to alert her to a message. When she had checked and saw that it came from Alex, she ignored it.

He was probably just letting me know he made it home OK. I'm glad, but right now that doesn't warrant a return call or a conversation. Especially when I know where that conversation is headed.

She sighed. Just when she thought she was making progress with accepting her own responsibility for her actions and moving in the right direction toward maturity, she realized she was more confused than ever. Despite his betrayal of her trust, hearing Alex's voice stirred her emotions and compounded her confusion, and she certainly wasn't up to dealing with that tonight. Besides, she needed time to digest all the thoughts and feelings that had risen to the surface during their visit to Bettina's house.

The dinner was beyond amazing, the people were warm and welcoming, and the conversation was pleasant and enjoyable. But there's more, isn't there, Lord?

As always, Megan was only slightly surprised to find her thoughts slipping into silent prayers. She'd been raised in a

Christian home, had become a believer herself while she was still in elementary school, and did her best to remember to make prayer and Bible reading a regular pursuit. But she had to admit that both practices were sporadic at best, so it was encouraging to her when she found herself spontaneously talking to God. And it seemed she'd been doing a lot more of that lately, especially since that last horrible date with Alex.

"Sometimes I wish You'd answer a little louder," she whispered. "I think You're using all the things that are happening in my life—especially today's dinner and even Mrs. Townsend's story—to teach me something. I just hope I don't miss whatever it is."

The hint of a word or a sentence darted through her mind, but she pushed it away, along with its accompanying sense of conviction. She knew she'd been wrong to abandon her boundaries and ignore all the warning signs that might have prevented her from ending up in her current situation, but it was too late now. She'd asked God to forgive her, and she knew He had. Now she needed to stay close to Him so she wouldn't continue to make such foolish choices in the future. As she did so often these days, she laid her hand on her stomach. Still flat. But for how long? She couldn't hide her condition forever; she was running out of time. Maybe she should call Alex back after all—

No. Net yet. It was nearing midnight, and she didn't want to risk waking his parents, even though she imagined he would have his phone on vibrate. Maybe she'd call him the next day . . . if he hadn't already called her back by then. She'd wait until after the planned lunch meeting with her mom and Mrs. Townsend.

The elderly woman's words about Elizabeth Blackwell drifted back in her memory, and she considered what the woman had endured as a child.

Cholera. Seasickness on a long ocean voyage to an unknown land. The continued, growing issue of slavery and abolition. How was it possible that a fragile child known as Little Shy could overcome so many obstacles and go on to achieve such notoriety and success?

Every medical student Megan knew, particularly the women, admired Dr. Blackwell. They had all read about and studied her life. So why did Megan feel as if she were hearing the story for the first time?

She sighed. Perhaps she would get her answer the following day. For now she really needed to try and get some sleep.

※　※　※

Jenny had been looking forward to leftover turkey all morning, but not nearly as much as she looked forward to sharing it with Laura and Megan.

"Thank You, Lord," she prayed aloud, as she put the tea kettle on and fluffed the sofa pillows, "for orchestrating all this. I never knew Laura well, though she seemed like a nice person, and I scarcely knew her daughter at all. But You stepped in and changed all that, didn't You? For the most part it may be for their sake, but I thank You for warming an old woman's sometimes lonely heart as well."

The bell on the front door tinkled, and she hurried out from behind the curtain to confirm that her company had arrived. Laura and Megan stood side by side, just inside the closed door, smiling at her and bearing bags full of goodies.

"Turkey sandwiches," Laura said, indicating her package. She nodded toward the bag that Megan held. "And cranberry sauce and pumpkin pie—not to mention the last of Megan's seven-layer dessert."

Jenny laughed. "It all sounds wonderful, but I can't imagine how you managed to salvage any of that delicious dessert of yours," she said, directing her words toward the younger woman. "Even with all the food to be had yesterday, your chocolate delight was a big hit, especially with the children."

Megan beamed. "It was, wasn't it? I actually meant to leave the rest of it there, but Earl insisted I take it home. Said they already had more than they could ever eat, and I'm sure that's true."

"No doubt," Jenny agreed. "Well, let's come on back and get started, shall we?"

In moments they were settled onto the old sofa, sipping tea and munching sandwiches, as they caught up on light chitchat before diving into the story.

"At least the weather has improved," Jenny observed. "It's still chilly out there, but the sun is out, melting what's left of the snow and ice. And I didn't see any predictions of more for the next few days."

"That's a relief," Laura said. "Megan has to return to school Sunday afternoon, and I'm a lot more comfortable knowing she'll be driving in good weather."

"I can imagine," Jenny observed, smiling at Megan before returning her attention to Laura. "So have you been busy at the clinic this morning?"

"Not too bad. Of course, that can change at any time, but if it doesn't pick up this afternoon, I just may be able to get home at a decent hour tonight. It would be nice to spend some quality time with my daughter before she has to leave."

Jenny caught the look Megan darted her mother's way, but couldn't read it. Was there something significant in the girl's wordless comment, or was Jenny letting her imagination run ahead of her?

"Well," she said, "are we ready to move on with our story?" She held up the quilt and quickly pointed out to Megan the patches they'd discussed so far; then she moved on to point out two other patches. One depicted a set of chains, the other a dollar sign.

"The meaning of the chains is obvious, isn't it?" Jenny commented. "We were talking about the Blackwells' growing involvement in the abolitionist movement. This had a huge impact on Elizabeth's developing personality and passions. Not only did she become an avid abolitionist, but she learned to identify with the hurting and oppressed, which helped drive her to the eventual vocation of providing medical care to those who were suffering and couldn't afford it."

She shifted her attention to the second patch now. "You may think it odd that I would include a dollar sign on a Christmas quilt, but if you remember correctly I told you there were two issues that loomed over the Blackwell household after their relocation to the new world. The first, of course, was their growing involvement in the abolitionist movement, which was at the heart of the country's unrest. The second was that the family was in financial trouble, and it was severe enough that it would impact them for years to come."

Interrupting herself, she rose to pour more tea but Megan beat her to it. "I'll get it. Please. You just go on with your story."

Jenny smiled at the young woman's thoughtfulness and nodded before she continued. "It started just before Christmas in 1835. A huge fire swept through the city of New York, compounded by the extreme winter weather that had dumped several inches of snow on the ground and prevented some firefighters from getting where they needed to be. There was little water to combat the flames, and though Samuel Blackwell joined many other volunteers in their valiant attempt to save their homes and businesses, it was nearly a futile endeavor. The Blackwells' sugar refinery survived, but with thousands of New Yorkers homeless and the economy gutted, Samuel realized his company could not survive for long.

"The situation went from bad to worse. By March 1837, Elizabeth wrote in her diary that she couldn't imagine what her papa's plans were for the future. Though she longed to help her family, she was, in her own words, 'only a female,' so what could she possibly do?"

Megan leaned forward, clutching her cup between her hands. "So what happened to them? Did they lose everything?"

"Very nearly." Jenny smiled. "But that starts the next episode of the story. Maybe we should stop at this point so your mother can get back to work."

Laura smiled and nodded. "Regretfully so, I'm afraid. I could sit here all day and listen, but I really do need to get back."

Jenny sensed Megan's disappointment and quickly jumped in with an offer. "Tomorrow at the same time? I usually open on Saturdays anyway."

Megan's expression brightened. "I'd love that." She turned toward Laura. "Mom? Will that work for you?"

"Absolutely. I wouldn't miss it."

Jenny's heart sang. *Thank You, Lord. Another day with my friends. You are so good to me!*

＊ ＊ ＊

LAURA HAD HEADED BACK TO THE CLINIC, leaving Megan to drive her own car back home. Even her mom had agreed that the weather was calm enough that the little "wannabe" vehicle should have no trouble making the short commute.

Megan's phone sat on the seat beside her, still blinking its red light. She had told herself she would call Alex if she hadn't heard from him by the time her lunch meeting was over. Well, it was over now. Should she call, or should she wait a bit longer? After all, the last thing she wanted to do was to give him false hope. That wouldn't be fair to him, and she doubted it would be a wise move for her. Sooner or later the two of them would have to talk, but she wasn't feeling quite ready for that conversation yet. Overall, she was leaning toward waiting until they both returned to school and could talk in person.

She reached out and flipped the phone over to mask the annoying red blink. If she wasn't ready to talk to Alex yet, what was the point of listening to his message? At least for the balance of the day, she was determined to ignore it.

Chapter 14

LAURA WAS PLEASANTLY SURPRISED to arrive home Friday evening and find Megan relaxing in one of the recliners in the family room. Flames crackled in the fireplace as Megan looked up and smiled.

"You made it home at a decent hour tonight. I wasn't sure when to expect you so I haven't really started anything for dinner yet."

Laura smiled and settled into the rocking chair across from Megan, immediately kicking off her shoes and sighing as she leaned her head back. "I'm in no hurry. In fact, I'm grateful for a few minutes to unwind first. Besides, we still have plenty of leftovers from yesterday. They'll only take a few minutes to warm in the microwave."

"My thoughts exactly." Megan raised her eyebrows. "Seems you got home fairly early, but you still look tired."

"I am." She leaned down and massaged her left foot. "We cleared out the waiting room on time today, but up until then it was nonstop all afternoon, ever since I got back from our lunch with Jenny." She looked up and smiled. "That was really my only break today, and I'm so glad you joined us."

Megan smiled. "So am I. I'm enjoying Mrs. Townsend's insights into Dr. Blackwell's life. I doubt there's a med student on the planet who doesn't know the basics about her, but I'm learning some interesting details that I don't remember hearing before."

"So am I," Laura admitted.

"You know that Dr. Blackwell was very much opposed to abortion," Megan said.

Laura felt a surge of heat rise from her neck to her cheeks, and she wondered at her reaction. "You're right. Though nearly everyone in the medical field or modern-day women's rights movement are quick to tout her pioneering work of helping women break into medical careers, few of them mention her strong pro-life stance."

Megan nodded. "It's almost as if someone can't be both a strong advocate for women as well as for unborn babies—which is ridiculous, of course."

Laura nodded. She agreed with everything her daughter was saying, and yet the discomfort that had precipitated her blush continued to nag at her.

"So," she said, changing the subject, "we're meeting with Jenny again tomorrow. But that's just lunch. What else do you have planned for the day?"

"Nothing much." Megan shrugged. "About like today, I guess. I'll hang around here and take it easy before I have to head back on Sunday."

"I feel so bad leaving you here alone all day. If I could break away from the clinic—"

"Mom, don't worry about it," Megan said, interrupting her mother's concerns. "I grew up with you, remember? I know about your dedication and long hours . . . and I'm fine with that. I came home to see you, yes, but also to rest and relax a bit." She paused, and Laura saw a twitch of anxiety flit across her face before she briefly dropped her eyes. "And . . . well, to talk to you about the baby too."

The warm flush was back, and Laura knew now that her discomfort had to do with the fact that she was still avoiding the in-depth conversation her daughter so obviously wished to have with her. She opened her mouth, ready to jump in and have the discussion once and for all, when Megan waved her off.

"I've thought about that a lot the last few days, and I've changed my mind. You and I really don't need to make all the long-term decisions together—not now, at least. There's plenty of time for that. Right now I'm just going to go ahead as planned and return to school until the end of the semester. By that time I'll have come to a decision about the next step." She fixed her eyes on her mother. "If that means leaving school for a few months—or longer, if necessary—and coming home until after the baby is born, are you OK with that?"

There it was. The question Laura had been dreading. Though she'd felt a twinge of relief that Megan didn't feel the need to pin down every detail of her future right here, right now, this weekend, Laura really hadn't wanted to face what Megan's predicament would mean to her continued education. Leave school for a few months—longer, if necessary? What was it about this possibility that bothered her so? Of course Laura would be heartbroken if Megan abandoned her medical career altogether, but there was no reason to think she would do such a thing. The thought that leaving the dream of becoming a doctor behind would hurt Laura more than Megan herself tugged at Laura's heart. Had she indeed pushed her daughter into pursuing a profession that wasn't truly what she wanted?

Ignoring that particular implication of Megan's question, Laura nodded. "Of course you can come here at the end of the semester—if leaving school then is what you think is best."

Megan's gaze lingered on her mother. "Thanks, Mom. I need to know that option is open if . . . if that's what I decide to do."

And what else could you do? The question shot through Laura's mind, even as she banished various answers. Marrying Alex was not an option; they'd broken up weeks ago, and he wasn't even aware of Megan's pregnancy.

Continuing on with school until she went full-term might be an option—if she felt well enough and was comfortable doing that. After that the decision would be whether to keep the child and raise it as a single parent, or give it up for adoption. The only other possibility—abortion—was not even a blip on their radar screen . . . was it?

Laura shook her head. Of course it wasn't. Neither of them believed in it. Laura had raised Megan to be strongly pro-life. Abortion wouldn't even cross Megan's mind.

Why then, Laura wondered, *had it crossed hers?* The thought both horrified and shamed her, and she resolved to banish it from her thinking, once and for all.

❋ ❋ ❋

JENNY HAD CLOSED THE SHOP and made the short trip home by midafternoon, when it became apparent she most likely wasn't going to get any more customers. As it was, no one had come in since Laura and Megan left after lunch.

Now, puttering around her little kitchen as she heated some cider and fixed a piece of toast for a light supper, she sighed at the realization of how much her little business had changed in recent years.

There was a time—and not that long ago—when the week-end after Thanksgiving launched my busiest selling season of the year. From there right through Christmas Eve, that little bell on my door tinkled every few minutes. Now it's nearly silent.

She sprinkled a hint of cinnamon on her toast. *It's the malls. People haven't stopped shopping; they've just stopped doing so in little stores like mine. It's easier to go spend the day at the mall and get everything done at once.* She sighed again, a bit louder this time. *Maybe everyone who tells me it's time to retire is right. But then what would I do with myself all day? I'd feel completely useless*

*just sitting around, watching TV or knitting slippers for people who
don't want them and won't wear them.*

She thought then of the many ministry opportunities at
her church and how she almost always declined them because
she had to be at the shop during the day. Maybe God was
telling her it was time to retire from the shop and to get more
involved in ministry of some sort.

The very thought stirred a longing in her heart, as she
sat down at the table with her toast and cider. "You know I'm
open, Lord," she prayed aloud, "if that's what You want me
to do at this stage of my life." She smiled. "And it would be
lovely to have more prayer and Bible study time. I never get
tired of being with You. In fact, I wouldn't be surprised if You
arranged this little get-together between us right now just so
I'd pray about something specific."

The memory of Laura and Megan sitting in her back
room at the shop crystallized in her mind. "Of course. There's
more to this storytelling about Dr. Blackwell than I know,
isn't there, Father?"

She took a sip of cider. "And I don't need to know,
so long as You do. All right, then, Lord. Let's talk about
those two dear women. You know I'm grateful to You for
bringing them back into my life, for however long and for
whatever reason. And You also know I'm perfectly willing
to tell Little Shy's story, particularly since I'm working on
my annual Christmas quilt with her life as my theme. But
whatever else is going on with those two ladies, I pray You'll
work it all out in Your time and in Your way, even if I don't
know what it's all about."

She took a bite of the slightly sweet toast and nodded.
It was a wonderful thing to rest in the promises of a faithful
God who never changes and whose promises are always true.
With that in mind, Jenny Townsend could continue to pray
and to trust her Lord for whatever the next day or season of
her life might bring.

✳ ✳ ✳

IT HAD TAKEN EVERY OUNCE of willpower Megan could muster to ignore Alex's call that Saturday morning. She considered at least listening to his messages, but hearing his voice—and possibly even his pleading—would make it that much more difficult to maintain her resolve to wait and talk with him face to face when they returned to school.

But now she was safely ensconced, once again, on the too-soft sofa in the back room of Jenny's Treasures, sipping tea and finishing her turkey sandwich while she waited for Mrs. Townsend to pick up their story where they'd left off the day before.

"Do you remember my telling you that the Blackwells were experiencing problems due to their strong abolitionist stance, as well as financial problems?"

Megan looked up from her sandwich, pleasantly surprised that the storytelling had resumed. She nodded. "I do, and I've been anxious to know what Elizabeth's father did to try to resolve the financial part of the problem."

"I've wondered the same thing," Laura said, placing her teacup on its saucer.

Jenny shook her head. "There was little to be done except to cinch one's proverbial belt, which the Blackwells certainly did. They were scarcely able to keep a roof over their head and any sort of food on the table. Of course, they weren't the only ones affected by the economic downturn. The country was experiencing a depression. Businesses failed, prices skyrocketed, and people rioted in the streets. In many ways, it was Bristol all over again."

Megan felt her eyes widen. She and her mother had experienced a few financial challenges after Megan's father and brother died, but they'd certainly never faced anything so dire as riots or a lack of food. Even with America's economic challenges of the last few years, Megan had to admit she'd never once been concerned over where she would sleep at night or what she would eat for her next meal.

"The Blackwell family had let their servants go and had even resorted to taking in boarders," Jenny said. "At night they couldn't afford to burn the lights in their home. At last Samuel announced that because his business ventures had failed, they were going to move to Ohio, where he believed they could do better, since theirs would be the only sugar refinery in that part of the country.

"The family auctioned off their furniture, shipped on ahead of them what few personal belongings they had left, and said good-bye to the city the Blackwells had come to love. As it turned out, the journey was nearly as dangerous and difficult as their crossing from England." She smiled and lifted up her quilt, pointing to a patch showing a tall, snowcapped mountain. "But they made it. They crossed the Allegheny Mountains and found themselves in what seemed another world, where people lived in log cabins along the riverbanks. At last their journey ended when they arrived in Cincinnati."

Megan felt a sense of relief. "Is that when things started getting better again for them?"

Jenny's face fell. "I'm afraid not. First, they discovered the depression they thought they'd left behind in New York had also invaded Ohio. Though they rented a house with the little money they had left, Samuel quickly learned it was not a good time to start a new business." She shook her head. "The family patriarch did everything he could to try to cover up how truly bad their situation was, taking the children on outings to explore their new surroundings and avoiding the topic of financial ruin, which loomed ever closer."

Jenny set her tea down and leaned forward slightly. "But the situation continued to deteriorate."

Megan couldn't imagine how much worse their situation could be, but she waited quietly to find out.

"Within a couple of months, Samuel Blackwell became very, very sick. The doctors referred to his condition as bilious fever, though no one really knew what that meant or how to treat it. The poor man continued to worsen, despite the bleeding techniques used by the physicians in a futile attempt to cure him. On August 7, less than three months after the family arrived in Cincinnati, he died."

Megan gasped. This was part of Dr. Blackwell's story that she hadn't known before. And yet, because of losing her own father, Megan could certainly relate. But something told her the Blackwell family had a much rougher time surviving financially after Samuel's death than she and her mother had.

"Little Shy had been so close to her father," Jenny reminded them. "On the day of the funeral, Elizabeth wrote that all hope and joy were gone, and she wanted only to die, as her father had done." She shook her head. "It was a very sad, dark day in the Blackwell family's life, particularly for Elizabeth."

Megan lifted her eyes and found her mother watching her. Their gazes locked, and Megan knew they were sharing the memory of their own grief. Yet it was obvious the young woman christened Little Shy by her beloved father had not given up. Instead, she pressed on to achieve formidable goals. As sad as Megan felt at the moment, she also felt inspired and encouraged.

But why am I not surprised that the amazing Elizabeth Blackwell first had to cross an entire ocean and a range of mountains, plus face heartbreaking loss, before she could even begin the journey to fulfill her life's purpose?

The thought brought both a stab of fear and a glow of encouragement to her heart.

Chapter 15

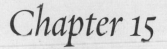

Saturday evening had been a pleasant time, as mother and daughter went out for a special meal together before returning home to chat over hot cocoa and cookies, finally falling into bed just before midnight. The best part, at least so far as Megan was concerned, was that they'd left the discussion of what to do about the baby on hold until the end of the next semester, though they had vowed to spend much time in prayer between now and then. As a result, Megan had dropped off to sleep almost immediately after her head touched the pillow. So far as she knew, she hadn't moved until the sound of the alarm on her cell phone woke her the next morning.

Fumbling on the stand beside her bed, she grabbed the phone and squinted at it as she turned off the annoying sound, accepting its offer of a five-minute snooze before sounding again. When the buzzing resumed, she shut if off for good and threw her legs over the side of the bed.

Church this morning, she told herself. *No matter how late you stayed up last night. Then a quick lunch with Mom before you hit the road.*

The thought brought an instant reminder that once she got back to school she was going to have to decide when, where, and how to approach Alex. *If he doesn't approach me first.* She picked up her phone to see if he had tried again to reach her.

Three missed calls! Wow. No doubt all from Alex. Should she finally cave in and listen to his messages? After all, hearing what he said might help her know better what to expect when they saw one another.

Heart racing, she punched the button for voice mail and waited. The first messages, recorded before she had actually talked with Alex earlier that week, were what she'd expected. She deleted them and moved on to the more recent calls.

"Megan?"

The woman's voice on the other end jarred her, and she sat up straight. Why would a woman be calling her from Alex's number?

"Megan, I don't know if you remember me, but this is Georgia Williams, Alex's mother."

The obvious fear in the woman's voice jacked Megan's heart rate up another notch.

"I'm calling because . . . because there's been an accident. Alex was . . . " Her words were interrupted by a sob, and then she continued. "Alex was hurt on his way home Wednesday afternoon—yesterday. He's in the hospital now, in and out of consciousness. When he's awake, he asks for you. We found his phone in the car, and since your number is in it, we—my husband and I—decided to try to call you. Please, if you get this message, will you call me? We're so worried about Alex. We're organizing a prayer vigil for him right now, but I can't help but think he might do better if he knew we'd talked with you. Better yet, if you could come here to Pueblo . . . "

Megan wasn't listening anymore. The woman's words had run together, and all she could think of was that the man she once thought had loved her—and she, him—and who was the father of her child was in a hospital, hanging between life and death.

He could even be dead by now, she thought, realizing the message she'd heard had been left on Thursday—Thanksgiving day. She listened to the others, updates from a heartbroken woman who still clung to the hope that her son was going to pull through.

"That means I'm not too late," Megan whispered, dropping the phone onto the bed and snatching some clothes from her semipacked suitcase. If she hurried, she could shower and be in Pueblo in slightly over an hour. She'd call Mrs. Williams along the way, assuming the woman still had Alex's phone with her, and let her know she was coming.

Megan made a beeline to the bathroom in the hallway, scolding herself the entire time. *Oh, why didn't I check those messages sooner? Why did I put it off?*

In moments she was standing under the steaming water, about to set a record for the world's quickest shower.

✻ ✻ ✻

LAURA FINISHED DRESSING and had just about made it down the hallway to the kitchen when she heard her daughter's bedroom door open behind her. She turned to see Megan hurrying toward her, suitcase rolling along behind.

"Megan, where are you going?" She frowned, standing her ground and forcing her full-steam-ahead child to stop directly in front of her. "I thought you weren't leaving until after lunch, and church isn't for nearly two hours yet. I was just about to make us some coffee and—"

Megan held up her hand and interrupted her mother midsentence. "Sorry, Mom. I can't go to church with you today. I can't even stop for breakfast. Alex has been in an accident. His mother called and—"

Now it was Laura's turn to interrupt. "Alex? An accident? When? How? What happened?"

"I don't know all the details. I just know from Alex's mom's messages that he was driving home Wednesday afternoon, during that storm, and . . . " She shook her head as her eyes filled with tears.

Laura's heart felt as if it were wrapped in the grip of that icy storm, as memories of another accident during another storm, on that very interstate, flooded her mind. "Oh, honey, I'm sorry," she said, reaching out to pull her daughter close.

Megan backed away. "Mom, there's no time. I don't know how bad he is, but I know from the messages that he asked for me when he was conscious. And they've got a prayer vigil going from their church, so it must be serious. Mom, I have to go. I *have* to."

Laura nodded. "Of course you do. But you're not going alone." She held up her hand to shush Megan's protests. "No arguments. Just let me get my coat and purse and we'll drive down there together. Have you talked to Alex's mother at all?"

Megan shook her head. "No. I just heard her phone messages. I was going to call her on the way."

"Good. You can do that while I drive. We'll grab some coffee on the way."

Megan nodded, and Laura knew her daughter was grateful for her support. Laura was just thankful she could offer it, since she felt as if she hadn't given much of it over the past few days. But underlying her sense of being glad to help her daughter was a distinct sense of unease at all that lay ahead.

❄ ❄ ❄

CLEAR WEATHER AND LIGHT SUNDAY MORNING traffic enabled the two women to drive to Pueblo in just under an hour. Megan managed to connect with Mrs. Williams via Alex's cell phone and confirm the name of the hospital. They pulled into the parking lot just after eight.

A blast of cool wind greeted them as they stepped out of the car, and Megan shivered as she drew her coat tight in front, resisting the urge to lay her hand on her stomach.

No, not now, she cautioned herself. *This is not the time to think about the baby and risk saying something. Even if Alex is conscious, he doesn't need any added stress. And I certainly don't want to mention it to his parents—or anyone else, for that matter.*

She glanced at her mother, who walked beside her, face solemn and straight ahead. Surely she understood not to say anything . . . didn't she?

"Mom?"

Laura turned her head briefly but kept walking. "What is it, honey?"

"I don't want to say anything to anyone about the baby. Not now anyway."

Laura nodded. "I know that, sweetheart. This is definitely not the time."

Megan felt a flood of relief ease the tension in her neck and shoulders. She should have known her mother already understood, but it was good to be certain.

As they arrived at the front entrance, the doors slid open and they stepped inside. Megan spotted an information desk to the right and headed in that direction. She'd spoken to Mrs. Williams only briefly and hadn't thought to ask for Alex's exact location.

In moments they had the information they needed and were standing in the elevator, making their way up to the third floor. Apparently Alex had been moved from the intensive care unit to his own room, and Megan imagined that meant he was doing better.

They stepped out of the elevator and looked at the room number signs and arrows on the wall. Megan was about to veer to the right when her mother laid her hand on her arm.

"Are you OK?"

Megan blinked back hot tears. "I think so." She shook her head. "To be honest, I'm not sure. It's not like Alex and I are still together. We're no longer a couple, but . . . even though he . . . even though we broke up, I still care what happens to him."

"Of course you do." Laura's eyes conveyed sympathy, even as her grip on Megan's arm tightened. "It's normal, regardless of where you two stand now or what, if anything, comes of your relationship in the future. Do you need a minute before we go to his room?"

Megan hesitated. "Do you . . . do you think we could find a restroom or something so we could pray first?"

Laura's eyes shone as she nodded. "I think that's a very good idea." She glanced from side to side and then pointed to the left. "There. Just a few steps down the hall."

Megan followed gratefully to the door marked Women, already thanking God that her mother had come along with her.

Chapter 16

LAURA LET MEGAN take the lead as they entered the room. A woman about Laura's age sat at the bedside, looking up the moment they entered. A tentative smile flickered across her face as she rose.

"Megan," she said, stepping toward them. "Thank you so much for coming."

Megan took the woman's outstretched hands and clasped them. "I'm just sorry I didn't come sooner. I should have checked my messages."

"No need to apologize. You had no way of knowing." She looked past Megan then, her dark eyes connecting with Laura's. "This must be your mother."

Megan, whose attention had already diverted to the still form in the bed, connected to tubes and wires and beeping machines, turned her attention back to Laura. "Oh yes, I'm sorry. Mrs. Williams, this is my mom, Laura Branson. Mom, this is Alex's mother, Georgia Williams."

Laura nodded and extended her hand in greeting, allowing her daughter to return her gaze to the man who lay motionless in the hospital bed.

"It's nice to meet you," Laura said, "though certainly not under these conditions."

Once again Mrs. Williams offered a weak smile. "True. But I think he's doing better. The doctor seems encouraged."

Slipping into physician mode, Laura asked, "What's the prognosis?"

Mrs. Williams's eyebrows lifted slightly before she answered. "Oh, that's right. I forgot you're a doctor, aren't you?" She glanced at her son before looking back at Laura. "He's had surgery to repair the broken bones in his leg, but the doctor is hopeful he'll heal up just fine from that. He also has some broken ribs, but thankfully no damaged organs. The big thing is the concussion he got when his head hit the windshield. But he seems to be coming around from that too. He's much more alert when he's awake now. The only reason he's still sleeping so much is the pain medication." She sighed. "I can't tell you how many times I've lectured him over the years about using his seatbelt." She shook her head. "He just wouldn't listen to me. Thought he was invincible, as so many young people do. Maybe this will show him otherwise."

Laura nodded. "I'm sure it will. And I'm sure he'll come out of all this just fine. Was anyone else hurt?"

"No, thank God. Alex collided with another car first and then a truck, but none of the drivers or passengers were hurt. It all could have been so much worse."

Laura realized she hadn't released the woman's hand after greeting her, so she squeezed it before letting go. "Yes, we're all thankful for that."

Her eyes darted to Megan, who sat in a metal folding chair beside Alex's bedside. Though her hands rested in her lap, her gaze was firmly fixed on the man in front of her.

"I'm so glad you both came," Mrs. Williams said, drawing Laura's attention away from her daughter. "We've had several people from the church here over the last couple of days, which was wonderful, and I expect some will drop by this afternoon after the service. But it's nice to have some company right now."

"Have you been here the entire time since they brought him in?"

Mrs. Williams nodded. "Nearly. My husband made me go home a couple of times to get some sleep, but I just ended up coming back after a few hours of tossing and turning. He's home resting now, but he'll be back soon, I'm sure."

"Has Alex been awake much this morning?" Laura inquired.

"Off and on. I imagine he'll wake up again before long—especially if he hears Megan's voice and realizes she's here. That seems to be his greatest concern."

Laura watched her daughter's reaction to Mrs. Williams's words. After just a few seconds she reached over to lay a hand on Alex's arm. "I'm here," she said, her voice scarcely above a whisper. "Can you hear me, Alex? It's Megan. I'm here."

❋ ❋ ❋

ALEX'S EYES FLUTTERED, right along with Megan's heart. What was she getting herself into? They'd made a clean break, a necessary one because of what he'd done, and they were moving on with their lives—until this.

That's not really true. You have a baby growing inside you—Alex's baby. That's not what most people would consider a clean break. You're tied to him for life now, no matter how this turns out.

Alex moved his head slightly in Megan's direction and moaned. His eyes fluttered again, this time opening into slits. They widened slightly as they focused on her.

"Meg—" The word was scarcely a croak, but it was obvious what he was trying to say.

"Yes, it's me, Alex. Megan." She leaned closer. "Can you hear me?"

He opened his mouth again, obviously struggling to voice his thoughts.

"Here," Mrs. Williams said, stepping up to the bedside and grabbing a pink plastic cup of water. She held it close to her son's face, guiding the straw into his mouth with her spare hand. "Take a sip," she said, waiting until he did. "Is that better?"

He nodded, wincing at the effort. His voice still cracked, but he seemed able to speak a few words now. "Thanks." He turned his eyes back to Megan, and a slight smile tugged at his lips. "You came."

Megan nodded, choking back a sob. "As soon as I knew. I should have been here right away, but I didn't check my messages."

"Doesn't matter," Alex whispered. "You're here now."

She took a deep breath. Yes, she was here now, but what did that mean? Quite obviously it meant something different to Alex than it did to her. She wanted to clarify for him that she had come only to support and encourage him, not to offer him an open door back into the relationship they'd had weeks earlier, but she knew this wasn't the time.

"Are you . . . doing OK?" She hesitated. "Better, I mean?"

"Better than when they brought me in," he answered, the effort showing in his eyes. "I'm getting better every day."

"I'm glad. But I think you need to rest. Go back to sleep. I'll be here when you wake up."

Alex smiled and closed his eyes. Apparently she'd said just the words he wanted to hear. And for now she imagined that was exactly what she needed to do.

❋ ❋ ❋

ALEX HAD DRIFTED IN AND OUT OF SLEEP two more times before noon, when his father rejoined them in the room. Reassured that Alex knew she was there and would return after a short break, Megan agreed to accompany her mother to the cafeteria to grab something to eat.

"Thanks, Mom," she said as soon as they were down the hallway. "I was feeling a bit tense and needed to get out of there for a while."

"Of course you did. So did I. We haven't eaten all day, and there's no need to stay there nonstop at Alex's bedside, especially with both of his parents there. I think they're expecting visitors from the church soon too."

Megan nodded. "Yes. Good time for a break."

They found the cafeteria and grabbed a couple of trays, browsing the offerings before making choices.

"We didn't have breakfast this morning," Laura said. "But I'm ready for lunch by now, aren't you?"

"I suppose, though I'm really not all that hungry."

"You need to eat. You won't do Alex or anyone else any good by starving yourself."

Megan surprised herself with a chuckle. "I doubt I'm in any danger of starvation, Mom. All I've done since I got home is eat."

Laura smiled. "We have done quite a bit of that these last few days, haven't we? I know I've eaten more than I normally do. But I must admit, I've enjoyed it—especially our threesome lunches with Jenny Townsend."

"Me too. I'm going to miss hearing her stories when I go back to school." She frowned. "I was supposed to do that this afternoon, wasn't I? Doesn't look like that's going to happen."

Laura stopped midreach for some fruit-covered yogurt. "Honey, I understand completely why you came today, but you're under no obligation to take up permanent residence here, you know."

Megan nodded. Her mother was right, but she felt guilty even considering leaving Alex behind in his current condition.

A man behind her in line cleared his throat, and Laura and Megan moved ahead with their lunch selection. Soon they were seated across from one another at a tiny table in the back corner. Megan eyeballed her vegetable soup and thought it didn't look nearly as good as the leftover turkey still sitting in her mom's refrigerator. The thought of sharing those leftovers with Jenny Townsend the past couple of days nudged her curiosity.

"Are you planning to have lunch at Jenny's Treasures again tomorrow, Mom?"

Laura raised her eyebrows. "Actually, yes, if at all possible. Why?"

"I'd like to join you for at least one more day before heading back to school. I could leave right after lunch tomorrow."

"I don't see why not, so long as you don't think it will be a problem to miss another day of classes. And I know Jenny would love it."

"Good." Megan was surprised that she suddenly seemed clear on what she wanted to do, at least for the next day or so. "Since Alex seems to be doing better, I'll stay with him the rest of the day and then let him know that I need to get back. His mom can call me if anything changes."

"I think that's a wise and practical solution. There's nothing you can do for him here except keep him company, and he seems to have plenty of that already."

Megan was glad her mother agreed with her plan. She imagined the only one who wouldn't was Alex. She would have to break it to him gently, assuring him that she would be in touch with his mother. *I'll tell him I'll be praying for him too. He really needs to know that. But I also need to be careful not to say anything to give him more encouragement about our relationship. No doubt he already thinks he's winning me back . . . but he's not. There are just way too many things that I don't think I can get past—well, at least one thing, anyway. And it's huge. But I have the perfect excuse for not telling him about the baby right away. He's getting better, but it's going to be a while before he's completely well. Until then, I'm keeping the news to myself.*

Her mother reached across the table and took one of Megan's hands, snagging her attention once again. "Shall we say the blessing so we can eat?"

"Good idea." She closed her eyes so her mother could pray. She still wasn't excited about eating the soup that sat cooling in the bowl in front of her, but she supposed she should at least give it a try. After all, there was another life growing inside her to consider now.

Chapter 17

MEGAN PULLED HER ROLLER SUITCASE down the hallway to her old bedroom, exhausted but relieved to be back at her mother's house.

I couldn't stay there another minute. It was just too stressful. Sitting there, watching Alex sleep or, worse yet, trying to encourage him when he was awake but without offering him false hope or expectations. I can only imagine what his parents must be thinking! Do they understand that we broke up and that he's seeing someone else?

She shook her head and flipped on the bedroom light, closing the door behind her. She and her mother had grabbed a quick bite to eat on the way home, and then both opted to go straight to bed. Megan knew her mother was at least as tired as she was.

I'm so glad she came with me, she thought, as she lifted her suitcase up and onto the bench at the foot of her bed. She unzipped it and snagged a pair of pajamas before yanking the comforter from her bed and pulling down the covers. *I would never have gotten through the day without her. But I'm still glad I decided to take more responsibility for my situation and not dump it all on her. She has enough to deal with. Knowing she's with me, whatever I decide, is enough.*

Taking just enough time to change into her pajamas and brush her teeth before turning off the light and climbing between the sheets, Megan allowed her mind to drift back to Alex. It was obvious he had not wanted her to leave, even suggesting she stay with his parents for a while, but she'd insisted she needed to return to school and would keep in touch with his mother for updates.

And I will. But I hope Mrs. Williams doesn't start asking any personal questions about our relationship. I'll have to answer them as honestly as possible, but that may mean omitting a lot of details for the time being.

Sowing and reaping—

The thought popped, unbidden, into her mind, and she winced. If ever she'd understood that principle, it was now. And the reaping seemed to continue growing, right along with the little life inside her womb. She imagined that if she were already happily married and sharing this waiting time with her husband, her thoughts would be geared toward simple things, like whether the baby was a boy or a girl. As it was, she wondered instead what would become of the child, being raised by a single mother. Is that really what she wanted for her baby . . . or for herself?

She sighed. She'd been taught that abortion wasn't an option, and how could it be if the life growing inside her was truly a human being? She'd always been so clear on that before, but now . . . no. Despite the implications of going ahead with the pregnancy, abortion was out, period. How could she ever live with herself if she sacrificed her child's life so she could pursue her own? That left single-parenting, the slim possibility of sharing parenting responsibilities with Alex . . . or adoption. None sounded ideal.

"What should I do, Lord?" she whispered into the darkness. "I know. I should have asked You that before I allowed myself to get into the situation that led to all this. But here I am now, and I can't go back and change things. But I do know You can take even our bad choices—our sins—and turn them around for good. I want that, Father.

I really do. I want to do the right thing, but I'm just not sure what that is."

No voice pierced the darkness that surrounded her, but a warm peace flooded her, and she relaxed. She still didn't know what she should do regarding Alex or the baby, but she was confident that God would show her in His time.

❋ ❋ ❋

MONDAY MORNING DAWNED CRISP AND CLEAR, with an icy wind slicing down from the mountains but no precipitation in sight. Laura was relieved. The last thing she wanted was for Megan to attempt the drive to Denver in a storm.

Patient traffic at the clinic was unusually slow for the beginning of a week, and Laura was glad. It made her planned lunch break easier to justify, at least in her mind. She still had a hard time getting used to the idea that she was actually entitled to leave for an hour each day, whether to eat or just visit with a friend—in this case, an old friend who was in the midst of telling her a fascinating story.

And my daughter too, she thought, snagging her purse and coat as she exited her office and headed for the front door via the nearly empty waiting room.

"My, my, this is getting to be quite a habit, isn't it?"

The sound of Bettina's voice reached her midstride as she passed the receptionist area. Laura turned and smiled at the woman who sat behind the desk, looking up at her. "It is, isn't it?" A pang of guilt stabbed her heart. "Do you think I should skip it today? I don't want to overburden Dr. Farmington."

Bettina waved her off. "He's fine. You go on. He'll take a break when you get back."

"Are you sure?"

She frowned. "Don't make me get up and come out from behind this desk. Now go on. You're wasting your hour. And trust me. We can get along just fine without you while you're gone." Her frowned morphed into a smile. "Say hello to Jenny for me."

Laura laughed and headed for the door. Bettina was right. She had to stop thinking of herself as indispensable. If she dropped dead tomorrow, the world really would go on spinning.

As she pulled up in front of Jenny's Treasures, she was pleased to see that Megan's car was already there. She had so enjoyed these last days with her daughter, even with the unexpected interruption of going to Pueblo the previous day. If only there were some way of knowing how all that would turn out, but of course there wasn't. It would be easier, though, if she didn't have to turn Megan loose today and watch her drive off to school.

Stop being such a control freak, she told herself, climbing out of her car and heading for the front door. *You're always telling everyone else to trust God and stop trying to manipulate circumstances. Maybe it's time to start practicing what you preach.*

The familiar tinkle announced her arrival at the shop, and Jenny poked her head out from behind the curtain. "I knew it was you. Come on back. Megan's already got the turkey sandwiches set out for us, and the tea is nearly ready. Oh, and don't forget to lock the door and turn the Closed sign out toward the street."

Laura followed the woman's instructions regarding the door and the sign and then made her way to the back of the store to join the two ladies for what she knew would be another pleasant and informative lunch together.

* * *

JENNY WAITED JUST LONG ENOUGH for Laura and Megan to get situated and start their lunch before jumping into the story. She knew it was the last time Megan would be with them, at least for a while, and she wanted to get in as much of Little Shy's life as possible.

"The day after Samuel Blackwell's funeral," she began, lifting the quilt to show the patch with the green dollar sign in the middle, "the family discovered he had left them a grand inheritance of twenty dollars. Even in those days, it wasn't much—certainly not enough to live on for any length of time. But it set the tone for what lay ahead for his widow and children."

Jenny watched the expected shock register on her guests' faces. Twenty dollars! What could a family be expected to do with such a paltry amount? And yet they had most certainly survived, and Jenny wanted the two women to appreciate that fact.

"Elizabeth had already begun giving piano lessons, even before her father died, and she went right back to doing so. The only other profession open to women at that time was teaching, so Elizabeth and her mother and aunt quickly advertised for pupils, and by the end of the month they had five students enrolled in their private school—held in their home, of course."

"That was quick," Megan observed, still holding half a sandwich in her hand. "But I can't imagine that five students could bring in that much income."

"True, but their enrollment increased quickly. Before long their school was prospering, so much so that Elizabeth and her mother had to scramble to keep up with their students, especially when Samuel's sister, Little Shy's Aunt Mary, died of the same illness as her brother. Sadly, Aunt

Bar also died soon after. The poor family scarcely had time to grieve their many losses. They had to push on just to keep the bills paid. But they did it, and life went on, as they say."

Laura shook her head. "I can't even imagine how hard all that must have been. Some of the children were still young, weren't they?"

Jenny nodded. "Far too young to work and help the family in any way. But they all pulled together and, somehow, survived those terrible years of loss and struggle. Elizabeth even did a brief stint in Kentucky, setting up and running a small school for girls. But she never felt at home there and was glad when the assignment ended and she was able to return home. The one thing that seemed to come out of her stay there was a reinforced commitment to abolition. Seeing the effects of slavery up close, as she did in Kentucky, was horrifying to her, and she came back to Ohio in August 1844, determined to fight it with every ounce of her strength." She paused before asking, "Would you like to hear a portion of what she wrote in a letter while she was there?"

Megan and Laura quickly agreed that they would, and Jenny picked up a piece of paper she had brought along for this very moment. Adjusting her reading glasses, she squinted a bit and began to read.

"I made a copy of it at the library over the weekend," she explained. "It's dated April 4, 1844." She read aloud.

I dislike slavery more and more every day . . . But to live in the midst of beings degraded to the utmost in body and mind, drudging on from earliest morning to latest night, cuffed about by everyone, scolded at all day long, blamed unjustly, and without spirit enough to reply, with no consideration in any way for their feelings, with no hope for the future—to live in their midst, utterly unable to help them, is to me dreadful, and what I would not do long for any consideration

. . . I do long to get hold of someone to whom I can talk frankly; this constant smiling and bowing and wearing a mask provokes me intolerably.

Jenny set the copy of the letter down on the coffee table. "For a young woman known as Little Shy, it sounds as if she was coming out of her shell and beginning to move forward into the courageous young woman she would soon become, don't you agree?"

The women most certainly did, and Jenny smiled in response. She was confident they were beginning to get a clearer picture of the historical Dr. Blackwell.

"So when did all this turn into a desire to become a doctor?" Megan asked.

Jenny's smile widened. It was exactly the sort of lead-in she'd been hoping for, and she was ready with an answer.

"Just a few months after her return from Kentucky, she was sitting at the bedside of a dying friend. The woman, whose name was Miss Donaldson, interrupted Elizabeth's chatter about various topics by laying her hand on her arm. And do you know what she said?"

Megan shook her head, her eyes wide.

"She said, 'Elizabeth, you're fond of study. You have health and leisure. Why not study medicine?' Now that was no casual comment—at least not in that day, when women not only didn't study or practice medicine, they didn't even discuss it. But this lady, who was dying of cancer, stressed to Elizabeth that she firmly believed she might not have suffered so severely if only she could have been treated by a woman. The concept was stunning to Elizabeth, who had never even considered such a thing."

"And now we take it for granted," Laura observed, shaking her head. "For some reason I just didn't pay much attention to the many details that led up to Dr. Blackwell's entry into the medical world of her day."

"Nor do most people. We hear how she broke the so-called glass ceiling of medicine, opening the field to women for the first time, but we don't grasp the struggles and hardships she endured to make that happen, nor do we hear much about her strong stand against abortion. I think we need to know those things if we're to appreciate what she accomplished."

And with that she picked up the teapot and refilled everyone's cup. They'd heard enough of the story for one day.

Chapter 18

MEGAN FOUGHT TEARS as she hugged Mrs. Townsend and her mother before exiting the store and climbing into her tiny car to start the journey back to school. She backed out of her parking space and turned her vehicle in the direction of the interstate, determined not to cry. So much of what she'd expected to accomplish during her visit had simply not occurred. Yet she felt full beyond anything she could have imagined, as if everything that needed to be done, had been—and then some, even if she didn't yet understand the reason for it all.

The details about Elizabeth Blackwell's life are a big part of it. It's amazing how little of her story I knew, even though her name is revered in medical schools, especially with us women students. But even Mom didn't seem to know a lot of the details that Mrs. Townsend shared with us.

As she drove out of town and neared the entrance to the interstate, she realized it was more than the simple details of Little Shy's life that had impacted her; it was the depth of struggle the young woman had endured and that shaped her for what she would face later.

"That's the part I really need to know, isn't it, Lord?" she whispered. "You're using her life to teach and prepare me for what's ahead, aren't You?" Megan smiled. She knew God did that sort of thing—often, actually—but never had it been so obvious in her own life. No doubt if she hadn't been dealing with such a future-determining issue right now, Elizabeth's story wouldn't be impacting her so strongly. With her future on the line—not to mention her baby's—each fragment of Little Shy's story seemed to influence her own choices and decisions. Megan supposed that was a good thing, as Dr. Blackwell was a woman to admire, but that didn't necessarily give her the clear-cut answers she needed when it came to the baby . . . and Alex.

Alex. Megan wondered how he was doing. She'd called Mrs. Williams this morning, and the woman assured her that Alex had rested well during the night and was continuing to improve. That was the news Megan had hoped to hear, and so she decided there was no need to check back, at least not until later in the day. After all, Mrs. Williams had her number and had promised to call if anything changed. For now, that was exactly the way Megan wished to leave it. She wanted to get back to school and back into the regular routine of her studies. Christmas would be upon them before they knew it, and Megan would once again be driving home for a visit with her mother. She could only wonder how things would stand between her and Alex by then.

❊ ❊ ❊

LAURA WAS AMAZED at how lonely she felt once Megan left. She thought she had long since gotten used to her "empty nest," but suddenly everything felt different. The house seemed to echo Megan's absence, but it was more than that. And Laura couldn't put a name to it.

She had bustled through the afternoon, staying busy with patients and getting caught up on reports. But now the day was over, and she was home alone. Even the leftovers from Thanksgiving had finally run out. Usually, by this time, she was tired of turkey and relieved to see the end of it. But tonight, its absence just added to her sadness.

Why should I be sad? What am I mourning? Megan is fine— pregnant, but fine. And I know she's safe and sound, back at school, because she called me when she got there. So what's going on?

She rummaged around the fridge and cupboards, nearly reduced to her previous, pre-Thanksgiving state of affairs, when the best she could scrounge up was a can of soup. Well then, soup it would be.

She pulled the can from the shelf and held it under the electric can opener, waiting until the whirring stopped before dumping the contents into a bowl and placing it in the microwave. Chicken noodle was hardly her favorite, but it was the only game in town tonight. At least there was a partial box of crackers, which Megan had picked up at the grocery store, so that might perk things up a bit.

With supper ready, she sat down at the table and stared at the bowl. She could think of several adjectives to describe it, but appetizing wasn't one of them. She pushed it away and nibbled on a cracker, propping her feet up on the adjacent chair and wishing Megan was sitting at the table with her as she'd been the last few days.

Megan. What is to become of you now? She blinked away tears and tried to swallow a bite of chewed cracker. *Now that you're pregnant. Now that you're unmarried and pregnant. Now that you're going to have to postpone your education—worse yet, discontinue it. This isn't what I wanted for you. Not what I wanted for you at all!*

The thought that what she'd wanted for Megan might not be what Megan herself had desired reappeared in her mind. She closed her eyes and let the tears spill over onto her cheeks. At least now she knew what she grieved and why she felt so overwhelmed with sadness. It was hard to watch dreams die, particularly when those dreams were for your only surviving child.

❄ ❄ ❄

"YOU MISS HER, DON'T YOU?"

Jenny's question caught Laura off-guard. She'd almost called to cancel their lunch, simply because Megan wouldn't be there to join them. But Bettina had practically run her out of the office, and so Laura had found herself sitting in Jenny's back room after all, sipping tea and pretending to enjoy the shrimp salads she'd picked up along the way.

Laura blinked before answering. "I do," she said, struggling to get the words past the lump in her throat. "More than I thought I would."

Jenny nodded and patted her hand but offered no words of comfort, for which Laura was grateful. Silence went best with the hand pat at this point.

"Would you like to hear more of Elizabeth's story?"

Laura hesitated. She would enjoy it so much more if Megan were here, but she wasn't. And she wouldn't be again, at least not until Christmas. She nodded. "Yes, I believe I would."

Jenny smiled. "I'm glad. Well then, let's pick up where we left off, shall we?"

She lifted the quilt from the arm of the couch and fondled a particular patch. "I'm making good progress on this quilt. I do believe I'll have it done soon, and certainly in plenty of time for Christmas."

"That's good. I'd almost forgotten that was your target date. Do you know who you're giving it to yet?"

"Not really. But I'm sure the Lord will let me know before it's finished." She smiled again, a bit wistfully this time. "Do you remember I told you that Elizabeth once said she didn't know what she would be when she grew up but she knew it would be something hard?"

Laura nodded. She did remember, and had thought about it often.

"Well, what could be harder than a woman breaking into medicine at a time when that simply was not allowed?" She extended the quilt to Laura, pointing out the patch with a black bag in the middle of it. "A medical bag," Jenny explained, "full of all sorts of instruments—and challenges, most of which Elizabeth hadn't even begun to imagine. In fact, the moment her dying friend suggested she study medicine, all Elizabeth could think of was how repulsed and squeamish she felt at the very idea. This was not something that had been a lifelong dream for the young woman. And one of the first people she mentioned it to, her abolitionist friend Harriet Beecher Stowe, told her the concept was completely impractical, pointing out to her that there wasn't a medical school in the country that would even consider admitting a woman. She went on to point out that even if she could gain entrance into a reputable school, it would cost money she didn't have. Finally, if by some miracle she managed to get the required education, how would she ever establish a practice? What patient would ever be examined by a female physician?" Jenny paused, allowing the questions to settle into Laura's thoughts before continuing.

"Though Elizabeth knew her friend's objections made perfect sense, they only served to strengthen her resolve to at least consider the option. She began to write to physicians she knew, asking what they thought. A handful replied that it was a grand idea, but an impossible one. It simply couldn't be done, and she would do well to abandon the hopeless pursuit. But the more negative responses she got, the more she dug in her heels and found herself determining to pursue this new challenge, whatever the outcome."

Laura smiled. "She was either the most courageous woman who ever lived—or the most stubborn."

Jenny chuckled. "Perhaps a little of both. And maybe that's what it takes to face such a formidable challenge head-on."

The expression on Laura's face told Jenny she'd hit a nerve. Maybe it was time to stop for the day.

Chapter 19

THOUGH SHE MISSED HER MOTHER and also Jenny Townsend's stories about Elizabeth Blackwell, Megan was relieved to be back at school and busy enough to keep from dwelling on Alex and the baby. Her morning queasiness seemed to be subsiding, and she was better able to concentrate on her studies now. She knew Mrs. Williams would update her on Alex's progress and alert her if there was a problem, so she was able to put that topic on the back burner as well—at least for now. By the middle of the week, it was almost as if her life had returned to normal, and she was grateful for that.

As normal as a med student's life can be, she told herself as she made her way across the campus toward her dorm. The biting November wind sliced through her parka, and she picked up her pace. Thick, dark clouds hovered overhead; no doubt the ground would be covered in snow by morning.

Not that it would make much difference, she reasoned, since she'd be inside studying all evening and then catching a few hours of sleep before racing to her first class early the next day. But busyness was good, and she welcomed the grueling schedule.

For the next few weeks anyway, she thought, mounting the steps to her dorm. She pulled open the heavy door and stepped inside, welcoming the warmth that greeted her.

Then it'll be time to head home again. She smiled at the thought of helping her mom decorate for Christmas but refused to give entry to the thought that Alex would be only an hour away, and quite possibly well enough to call her and push for a visit. Since she'd raced to the hospital when she'd heard he was injured, how would she bow out of a visit once he was improving?

She climbed the stairs to her room and decided that maybe she wouldn't even try to get out of seeing him. If Alex seemed strong enough by then, she'd break the news to him about the baby and see how he reacted. She couldn't put it off forever, so why not get it over with during the two-week break from school? Though she had no idea when Alex would be up to returning to classes, she knew he'd show up sooner or later. Maybe it would be better if he had some time to process the news before they crossed paths on campus.

With that thought in mind, she let herself into her room, greeted her already-studying roommate who, thankfully, was using earbuds to listen to her ever-present blaring music, and tossed her things on the small desk by her own bed. It was time to put personal issues out of her thoughts and focus on her studies. She couldn't imagine how anyone could study with music blasting directly into their eardrums, but Megan had a quiz tomorrow, and that left no room for speculating or mind-wandering.

❄ ❄ ❄

THURSDAY MORNING BROKE COLD AND WHITE, with patients trickling into the clinic's waiting room at a slower than usual pace. Since the streets had been plowed and it seemed the storm had broken, Laura decided to keep her regular lunch date with Jenny. When she stepped through the door into the shop, her friend responded to the tinkling bell by emerging from behind the blue curtain and greeting her with a broad smile.

"I'm so glad you came. The way the snow came down last night, I wasn't sure if you would. It seems much better now, though, doesn't it?"

Laura nodded. "Definitely. The streets are clear, and not a falling snowflake in sight." She held up a large white bag. "I brought soup again. Vegetable. It was the only thing I could think of when I walked out the clinic door and got blasted by the frigid air."

"Vegetable soup sounds perfect," Jenny declared before giving her usual directions about locking the door and flipping the sign. "Come on back. The tea is all ready for us."

Both women were settled in and warming themselves with tea and soup, as Laura anticipated the next installment of Dr. Blackwell's story.

"You know," Jenny said, interrupting Laura's thoughts just as she swallowed the last of her soup, "I've been thinking about Little Shy's reaction to her friend's comments."

Laura raised her eyebrows and set her empty soup container on the coffee table.

Jenny smiled. "I'm sorry. I should have been more specific. I tend to speak out on my thoughts without realizing you haven't been tracking with those thoughts the way I have." She chuckled. "I was referring to Harriet Beecher Stowe's negativity toward Elizabeth's mention of studying medicine and possibly becoming a doctor someday."

Laura nodded. She was back on-track with Jenny's story now. "If I remember correctly from my sketchy studies of Dr. Blackwell years ago, she simply used every naysayer and obstacle as an impetus to dig in her heels even deeper and plow ahead."

Jenny's blue eyes sparkled. "Exactly! What had been little more than an idea rolling around in Elizabeth's mind quickly became a challenge to overcome when her friend declared it could not be done. Though there were a few small schools on the periphery of accepted medical practices that occasionally admitted a handful of women, Elizabeth wasn't about to settle for anything but a complete medical education. And that, of course, was the problem. Not one medical school in America would even consider admitting a woman."

"Most anyone would have given up at that point," Laura observed, refilling her empty teacup.

Jenny smiled. "And even the indomitable Miss Elizabeth Blackwell might have done the same—except for a powerful spiritual experience that strengthened both her Christian faith and her determination to become a doctor."

Laura frowned. "I vaguely remember that, just as I vaguely remember that Dr. Blackwell was strongly pro-life."

"Neither point is stressed in secular education or books," Jenny agreed, nodding. "But both are vital in understanding this courageous woman's life." She sipped the last of her own tea and smiled a thank-you when Laura refilled her cup.

"Little Shy's first step in moving toward becoming a physician was to raise the $3,000 it would cost for her necessary schooling—even though she had no idea where she would go for that schooling once she had the money. But $3,000 was a huge amount in those days, and the Blackwells certainly didn't have it. So she accepted a teaching position in Asheville, North Carolina. The decision required a grueling trip by horse-drawn wagon and a heart-wrenching good-bye to her family. It wasn't until she arrived in Asheville that the loneliness overwhelmed her and she wondered if she was indeed tackling the impossible."

Laura shook her head as Jenny paused for another sip of tea. "I hadn't thought of the loneliness aspect of what she was up against. She had no husband or children, and now she was separated from her mother and siblings too."

Jenny nodded, replacing her cup in its saucer. "She most certainly was." She caught Laura's eye and smiled. "But she wasn't separated from her God. As she wrestled with her fears that first night in her room, far away from everyone she knew and loved, she cried out, 'Oh God, help me! Support me! Lord Jesus, guide, enlighten me!' She later said a glorious presence flooded her at that moment, driving out all fear and despair, assuring her that she was indeed fulfilling her purpose in life. Though her hardships had only begun, her doubts were dispelled in that moment, and she pressed ahead with fresh determination and faith."

Laura smiled and nodded, her tea forgotten as she considered this powerful turning point in Elizabeth Blackwell's life. Searing the thought to her memory, Laura determined to call her daughter that evening and share this particular part of the story with her. Something told her they would both need to cling to it in the weeks and months to come.

❋ ❋ ❋

MEGAN SPENT SEVERAL HOURS TOSSING AND TURNING, twisting around in her sheets and blankets, wondering how far into Friday it would be before she finally drifted off. It was a good thing she'd taken her exam Thursday morning and didn't have an early class the next day.

Mom's phone call. It was good to hear from her and to know how well her visit with Mrs. Townsend went. But that part about Elizabeth Blackwell's spiritual experience confirming her determination to move forward—

I know Mom meant it to encourage me, but somehow it just made me feel guiltier than ever. I sure haven't had an experience like that with God—not since I was a little girl and first accepted Christ at summer camp. But I was innocent then.

A warm tear slid down her cheek and landed in her hair. True, she had begun praying and talking with God again lately, and she was glad for that. But innocent? She was far from it. Regardless of the part Alex had played in their relationship, particularly the night their child was conceived, she could not claim innocence. Looking back, she knew now that God had been warning her, cautioning her against moving ahead in a relationship that wasn't built on a godly foundation. She had thought she could handle it. She was wrong.

More tears followed the first one, until her hair and pillow—and even her ears—became wet. Sadly, she couldn't tell if she was crying for the innocent child growing within her—or the innocent child she had once been and who now seemed lost forever.

Chapter 20

ALEX AWOKE MIDMORNING ON FRIDAY, feeling slightly more clearheaded than he had since the accident. A quick glance around the room confirmed that he was still in the hospital, and the cast on his leg and pain in his chest when he tried to breathe assured him that he had indeed been seriously injured.

He frowned, trying to concentrate. An accident? Yes, that was it. Vague memories of driving in a bad storm, a simultaneous jolt to his vehicle and a flash of red to the side, the thought that he should have worn his seat belt . . . all came together to paint an unfinished picture of how he had ended up here.

Megan.

Images of her face, her voice, danced through his mind, and he smiled at the realization that she had come to see him. *She still cares. I knew she did.* His eyes darted around the room again. Where was she now? Why wasn't she here? And his parents? He knew they'd been here almost nonstop the last few days, even if the memories were vague. Where had everyone gone?

As if in answer to his silent question the door to his room pushed open and a familiar face peered inside. The middle-aged man with the short, graying hair smiled when their eyes met.

"Alex." He stepped into the room, letting the door close behind him. "It's good to see you awake. How are you feeling?"

The pastor of Mom and Dad's church . . . our church, he thought, searching for the man's name. "I'm fine," he responded, then caught himself as a searing pain jolted his chest. He grimaced. "Well, maybe not fine. If I remember right, Mom said something about some broken bones."

The pastor nodded and approached Alex's bedside, pulling up a chair to sit beside him. "A broken leg and several ribs, not to mention a concussion." He smiled again. "Could have been a lot worse. You had a lot of people worried."

Alex nodded, though even that small effort brought discomfort. "I know. I feel bad about that."

"Don't." He laid a hand on Alex's arm. "We're all just glad you're doing better. We've been praying."

"I know that too. And I appreciate it."

"This is the most alert I've seen you, and I've been here several times over the last week. I'm encouraged at your progress."

Alex raised his eyebrows. "Week? I've been here a week?"

"Longer, actually. The accident happened Wednesday afternoon, on your way home for Thanksgiving weekend."

Ah, now the missing pieces were falling into place. But . . . he'd missed several days of school? With his shaky grades, that couldn't be a good thing.

"What day is it?"

The pastor smiled. "Friday." He glanced at his watch. "Just about ten thirty in the morning."

Before Alex could respond, the door opened and a nurse peeked in, her glance stopping on the man in the chair.

"Sorry." She smiled, still hovering in the doorway. "I didn't realize our patient had company, though I believe I've seen you here before."

"Yes, several times," he said, starting to rise before she waved him back to his seat. "I'm Pastor Stafford. I just dropped by for a quick visit and a word of prayer."

"Of course. I remember now. Don't get up, Pastor." She shifted her glance from the pastor to Alex. "I'll be back to check on you in a little while. Do you need anything?"

Alex resisted the urge to shake his head, reminding himself not to make any unnecessary moves. "Nothing right now, thanks."

She nodded and stepped back out of the room, leaving the door shut once more.

Stafford. Pastor Stafford, Alex thought. *I need to remember that.*

"So, Alex, shall we have that word of prayer before I take off and leave you in the capable hands of the medical staff?"

Alex blinked, surprised at the question. Pastor Stafford was smiling, but Alex knew he was serious about wanting to pray for him. What should he say? He wanted to get better, of course, and he supposed he could ask for prayer for that. But was there something else, something less obvious but just as relevant?

He immediately thought of Megan, but he wasn't sure he wanted to get into that with the pastor, though he wouldn't mind God's help in getting that mess straightened out. Still, he couldn't imagine that God would answer a prayer like that, especially after what Alex had done to get everything to the mess it was in now.

"I . . . " He opened his mouth, knowing he needed to say something but still drawing a blank on what it should be. Then he remembered the times he'd heard people in church ask for "unspoken prayer" requests. He hadn't thought much about it until now, but if he understood it correctly this might be the perfect way to handle the pastor's question.

"I . . . actually do have something," he said, feeling guilty even as he spoke. "But it's . . . kind of private. Sort of an unspoken request."

Pastor Stafford nodded. "I understand, and I'll be happy to pray that way." He took Alex's hand in his, closed his eyes and bowed his head. Alex did the same, though he remained silent as the pastor petitioned God on his behalf. Did Alex dare to hope that God might actually listen . . . and answer? If He did, Alex knew it wouldn't be because he deserved it. But didn't the church preach a lot about God's mercy? Yes, they did, and in this case, Alex was banking on it.

※　※　※

THEIR FRIDAY LUNCH of tuna salad and breadsticks nearly consumed, the two ladies relaxed against the soft back of the old sofa behind the blue curtain in Jenny's shop. Laura was pleased when Jenny dived right into the story the moment she set her teacup down on her saucer.

"You know, in addition to earning some of the much-needed money Elizabeth needed for medical school, she established some good friendships and connections while teaching in North Carolina. In fact, her time there would have been rather pleasant if she hadn't found herself even more deeply disturbed by the slavery she witnessed firsthand."

Laura nodded. "Her abolitionist views seemed to be an ongoing theme in her life, didn't they?"

"Most assuredly. As did her pro-life stance, though again, that is not as well-known as her stand against slavery. As a matter of fact, the misconception that any female involved in most any area of the medical practice at that time was an abortionist caused Little Shy a lot of grief."

"I can imagine."

"Still, while teaching in North Carolina, she spend every spare minute reading and studying medical books. When the school in Asheville closed, Elizabeth was invited by her landlord's brother to come to Charleston, South Carolina. This man, who happened to be a physician, had learned of Elizabeth's desire to enter the medical profession. He explained to her that he would not be able to get her into a medical school, but he did promise to find her some sort of job and to personally direct her medical studies while she was there." Jenny leaned forward, her eyes sparkling. "You can imagine how quickly she accepted his offer."

Laura chuckled. "I can, yes. It sounds like a great opportunity, considering the circumstances at the time."

"Exactly. She quickly went back to teaching during the day, while studying medicine and Greek far into the night. She saved every penny possible, keeping her eyes firmly fixed on her goal. This went on for approximately eighteen months, until she received an invitation from a doctor in Philadelphia to come and discuss her plans with him. Though he made her no promises, she was encouraged and accepted his invitation, particularly since Philadelphia was considered the center of American medicine at that time."

She paused and poured herself another cup of tea, offering one to Laura, who declined with a shake of her head.

"How are we doing on time?" Jenny asked.

Laura glanced at her watch. "I can stay a few more minutes."

Jenny smiled and nodded, picking up the quilt and pointing to a patch with what appeared to be a large bell on it. "Good. This patch represents the Liberty Bell and Elizabeth's time in Philadelphia." She set the quilt down in her lap and continued. "When she arrived in Philadelphia, she boarded with a man named William Elder, a Quaker who was also a doctor and a countercultural thinker. When she went to see Dr. Warrington, the physician who had invited her, she quickly won him over with her gentle but firm determination. He gave her permission to sit in on his lectures and even to accompany him when he visited patients. He also allowed her to use his well-stocked library and went so far as to check into the possibility of helping her gain admission into medical school."

Laura frowned. "That was very kind and supportive of him, but if I remember correctly, he wasn't successful in his efforts."

"I'm afraid not. However, she soon met another doctor, Jonathan Allen, who helped her with private studies of anatomy, being sensitive to her Victorian upbringing and starting with the wrist so she wouldn't be repulsed. Remember, she was more than a bit queasy when it came to human anatomy, which was quite natural in her day. Anyway, this time of study was very influential in helping Elizabeth move on to the next level in her studies. She quickly progressed from books to anatomical models and then to cadavers. And she continued to expand her relationship within the medical community, as respect for her grew." She sighed and shook her head. "But none of that made a whit of difference when she tried to gain admittance to medical school."

"I can't even imagine her frustration," Laura commented. "I sometimes wonder how she continued on in the face of such resistance."

"I often wonder that too, though I remind myself that she believed she had a mandate from God Himself."

Laura nodded. "True. That must have been a huge part of why she stuck it out and eventually succeeded."

"One doctor told her the only medical school that would ever accept her was in Paris but that she shouldn't even think of applying there because the city was far too 'wicked.' Another said she could come and study at his college if she dressed as a man. Of course she refused both offers. She wanted to practice medicine in America, not in France, and she wanted to do so openly as a woman so she could pave the way for other women to follow."

"And I, for one, am very grateful for that."

Jenny smiled. "Of course. But poor Elizabeth, who was nearly twenty-seven by then, found herself fighting despair. It seemed there wasn't a medical school anywhere in America that would even consider her. And then the letter came."

"The letter of acceptance." Laura returned Jenny's smile. "That much of her story I remember."

"Yes. The letter from the dean of the faculty at Geneva Medical College of Western New York."

Laura laughed. "That was always one of my favorite parts of Dr. Blackwell's story. To think that she was admitted by a vote of the student body—who voted in her favor because they thought it was some sort of joke—makes me want to laugh and cheer at the same time."

"Most definitely. Though, of course, Elizabeth had no idea at the time that she'd been voted in by mistake. All she knew was that she was heading for medical school—at last."

✳ ✳ ✳

MEGAN WRAPPED UP classes early on Friday and wandered back to her dorm room, enjoying the unseasonably pleasant weather as she crossed the campus. Weather reports predicted sunshine and temperatures in the mid 50s all weekend, and she knew it was going to be tough to stay inside and study.

She climbed the stairs to her room and heard music seeping through the door before she even had her key out. *Ugh. Lindy's in one of her "I need music to concentrate" moods again, and this time she isn't using her earbuds. Glad it works for her, but it sure doesn't do anything for me.*

Rummaging in the bottom of her purse, she scooped up her key and was about to insert it in the lock when the thought occurred to her that she could undoubtedly get more studying done at home than on campus. The weather was perfect, so there really wasn't any reason to be concerned about the relatively short drive to the Springs. Why stay here, cooped up in a tiny room and trying to block out Lindy's music all weekend, when she could study in the peace and quiet of her room at home?

Smiling, she unlocked the door and stepped inside, ready to throw a few things in her suitcase and head for the freeway.

Chapter 21

"HI, MOM. I'M HOME!"

The familiar words ignited a warmth in Laura's chest as she turned from the kitchen counter where she'd been chopping vegetables for a salad, eagerly anticipating her daughter's impromptu visit.

Megan appeared in the doorway, and Laura quickly met her halfway across the kitchen, pulling her into an embrace. "I'm so glad you're here, sweetheart." She pulled back and looked into her wide green eyes. "Is everything OK? I didn't expect you back before Christmas."

"I know." Megan's smile faded only slightly and she shrugged. "It was a last-minute decision. My roommate's music was blasting, I had a ton of studying to do, and . . . I don't know. It just seemed like a good idea at the time. That's when I called you and jumped in the car."

Laura laughed. "I'm so glad you did. How was the drive?"

"Uneventful." Megan pulled away and unzipped her parka. "It's chilly out, but no snow in sight." She slid out of her jacket and retrieved the small roller suitcase she'd left sitting in the kitchen doorway. "I'm going to go deposit this in my room. I'll be right back."

"Good. Dinner will be ready in no time. I'm glad you called ahead so I could get started on it before you got here."

"You didn't have to," Megan called from the hallway. "But I'm glad you did; I'm starved!"

Laura smiled and went back to her task. The tuna casserole bubbled in the oven, nearly done, and the salad was almost finished too. It wasn't often that Laura cooked anymore, but she was happy to do so for a special occasion like an unexpected visit from her daughter. *It's a good thing the clinic was slow this afternoon and I got home early or I wouldn't have had time to do this.*

"Anything I can help with?"

Laura blinked, surprised that Megan had returned so quickly. She turned. With her jacket off, Megan looked trim and healthy. *Did I expect otherwise? She's only a couple of months along and won't be showing for a while yet.*

"You can set the table. Everything else is nearly ready."

Megan smiled, her cheeks still flushed from the cool air outside, and quickly retrieved the necessary plates and silverware.

"So you said you have lots of studying to do," Laura commented, adding the last of the chopped veggies to the salad. "Does that mean you'll need to spend most of the weekend in your room?"

"Some of it, but not all. I'll hit the books tonight and for a few hours in the morning, but if you're having lunch with Mrs. Townsend I'd love to join you."

Laura raised her eyebrows as she carried the salad to the table. "I am, as a matter of fact, and it would be wonderful if you came along. Jenny will be pleased too."

Megan nodded as she arranged the place settings. "I look forward to hearing more of her stories about Dr. Blackwell. Have I missed much?"

"Not really." Laura opened the oven door and checked the casserole. Perfect. Using potholders, she pulled it from the oven and carried it to the table, setting it on a silver trivet beside the salad. "I'll fill you in while we eat, and then you'll be up to speed for tomorrow."

"Sounds good." Megan smiled. "I'm so glad I decided to come."

"So am I." Laura leaned toward her daughter and kissed her on the cheek. Then they sat down and offered a prayer of thanks before digging in.

* * *

JENNY WAS DELIGHTED that Megan had joined them, but it confirmed her sense that something was amiss. She would continue to pray.

"The tuna casserole is delicious," she said, smiling at the two women who had joined her on the sofa. She laid her fork across her nearly empty plate. "But I'm afraid I can't eat another bite."

"I'm full too," Laura agreed. "Is it just me, or is casserole better the second day?"

"It's great both times," Megan said, still eating. "I loved it last night, and I love it today. You two don't mind if I have another scoop, do you?"

Jenny chuckled as she watched the young woman help herself to more lunch. Ah, to be young again and have such a healthy appetite!

"While you eat, I'll go ahead with the story," Jenny said. "I know your mom is on a bit of a tight schedule."

"Please do," Megan said between bites. "I know Mom has to get back to work, and I have to get back home to study. Meanwhile, I want to hear as much of the story as possible. Mom filled me in on what I've missed this week, so go ahead and pick up where you left off with her."

"Perfect," Jenny agreed, lifting the quilt and pointing to the square that sported what appeared to be an old-fashioned schoolhouse. "So you know, then, that Little Shy had been nearly miraculously accepted into medical school."

"Sort of—something about her being voted in by mistake, but I don't remember the story well enough to be sure what that means."

Jenny laughed. "Elizabeth didn't know what it meant either. She didn't find out until after she'd arrived and begun her studies that the school officials had been horrified by her application and saw it as a potential political problem. She was certainly qualified and had an influential sponsor in Dr. Warrington, so they were looking for a way out. They decided to submit her application to the entire student body and let them vote. Since all the students were male, they had no doubt she would be rejected outright. However, the students thought it was a joke and responded accordingly, unanimously voting her in. The next thing she knew, she was on her way to Geneva Medical College in New York. Of course, by the time she arrived for her first day in class, the students had forgotten their vote to admit her and were shocked when she actually showed up."

Laura shook her head. "I can't even imagine how she felt, walking into a classroom full of male students whom she thought supported her, since they'd voted her in."

"Their stunned expressions must have been quite confusing for her," Jenny agreed. "But she immediately got to work, taking notes, studying into all hours of the night, performing well on exams, and slowly making grudging points with her fellow students. But her time there was extremely lonely. Not only was she the only female student on campus, but the other boarders where she rented a room, as well as the vast majority of the citizens of Geneva, avoided her as if she were some sort of circus oddity. Her letters from home were one of her few comforts, and she clung to them as she devoted every spare moment to her studies."

Jenny took a sip of tepid tea before warming it with a fresh fill-up. "Word of her admittance into medical school quickly spread around the country. Newspapers wrote articles about her, many of which were unflattering and condescending. But she didn't allow it to deter her. Little Shy was more determined than ever to complete her studies. What she would do after that remained a mystery, but she would deal with that obstacle when she came to it."

"She had very little financial support during this time, am I right?" Laura asked.

"It was nearly nonexistent," Jenny explained, observing the admiration in her guests' eyes as they began to grasp the depths of Elizabeth's hardships. "There was nothing left over for new clothes or perfume or evenings out. Everything went to her studies. She was completely dedicated."

Laura shook her head. "It shames me to realize how much I take for granted, how little I truly sacrifice for my profession, and how much I owe to people like Dr. Blackwell, who went ahead of me and paid the price."

"I'm only beginning to understand that too," Megan agreed, at last setting her fork down on her now empty plate. "Maybe that's why this story fascinates me so much. It really helps put things into perspective." She cast a glance at her mother, who sat beside her, their eyes connecting. "Everything, even those things that don't have to do with medicine and becoming a doctor."

Laura nodded, and Jenny realized that whatever she had sensed was going on beyond the obvious was common knowledge between them.

As it should be, she thought. Aloud she said, "This seems a good place to stop for the day. I wish you could be here to share the rest of the story next week, Megan."

"I wish I could too. But I need to get back to school tomorrow evening."

The ladies stood and began to collect their things, as Jenny made a silent vow to continue praying for both of them.

* * *

MEGAN HAD MANAGED TO FINISH her studies Saturday night and enjoyed attending the Sunday morning service with her mother.

"Have you got time to stop for a quick bite of lunch with me before you head back?"

Laura's question was perfectly timed for Megan's musings. "To be honest, Mom," she said, as they headed to the parking lot where their two cars were parked side by side, "I think I'm going to hold off on driving back to school until much later this afternoon."

"Really?" Laura raised her eyebrows, obviously surprised by her daughter's announcement. They stopped between their cars, their coats buttoned against the biting wind. "I don't suppose that's a problem weather-wise, as I haven't heard anything about snow for the next few days, but you brought your suitcase with you this morning, so I assumed you'd be leaving soon. Why the sudden change of plans?"

Megan dropped her eyes, feeling the warmth climb from her neck to her cheeks. Would her mother understand her decision?

"It isn't actually sudden," she explained, lifting her gaze. "I've been thinking about it since I got here Friday night." She paused before plunging ahead. "I've been staying in daily contact with Alex's mom, plus he's called a couple of times too. He's home now and doing better. I thought I might drive down there for a quick visit before heading back. Would you . . . like to come with me?"

Megan watched her mother's face as she waited for her reply. She knew it made no sense for her to visit Alex now that they were no longer a couple and he was out of immediate danger, and even less sense when she allowed herself to consider the details of the story her mother didn't know. And yet there was a part of her that still cared, though she wrestled with admitting it even to herself. She wouldn't dream of confessing it to Alex—not now and maybe never—but she knew her concern went beyond the fact that Alex was the father of her child.

"I'd be happy to go with you," her mother answered, smiling. But Megan had seen the doubt flicker through her eyes even as she spoke.

"Thanks, Mom. Which car should we take? We can leave the other one here and pick it up when we get back."

Laura's smile appeared more genuine this time. "Let's take mine. It's roomier, and much less apt to blow off the road in this wind."

Megan laughed. "Deal. I'll drive. And we can pick up some lunch on the way."

Chapter 22

THE WIND WAS STILL KICKING UP BUT, as promised, still no hint of snow as they pulled up in front of the Williamses' home. Though Megan had been there once, she'd had to punch the address into her mom's GPS to find it, as Alex had been driving when they came before and she hadn't paid much attention to how to get there.

Alex's mother had been pleased when she'd called to say they were coming. "I just got home from church," she'd said after answering the phone. "My husband stayed home with Alex so I could go. We want to be sure someone is with him all the time, at least for now."

Megan had agreed that it sounded like a good idea, since Alex no doubt still had a long way to go before he'd be able to get around and do much on his own. She imagined his macho persona was irritated by that, while at the same time he probably enjoyed his parents' waiting on him.

That's because he's so immature, she reminded herself. *Hardly a good candidate for fatherhood.*

And yet, whether he actively participated in their child's future or not, he was indeed going to be a father. When and how she would tell him about that was a question she had yet to answer.

She was relieved for her mother's sake that they didn't have to wait long after ringing the doorbell. The temperature had dropped considerably over the weekend, despite the pale sunshine overhead. But when Mrs. Williams opened the door, Megan was immediately struck by how weary she looked. The lines on her face seemed to have multiplied, as well as deepened.

"Come in," she said, smiling as she stepped back to let them pass. "It was so nice of you both to drive down. Alex was excited when I told him you were coming."

Megan swallowed the lump that swelled in her throat. Had she been wrong to come? Was she offering false hope to Alex? True, she'd been less than an hour away at her mother's home, but Alex hadn't known that. She could easily have driven straight back to school after church and he would never have known about it. But she hadn't. Was she being honest with herself about her motives for visiting?

"He's in his room," Mrs. Williams went on. "Last time I peeked in, he was awake and waiting for you. Please, follow me."

They did, and in a matter of seconds found themselves standing at the foot of Alex's bed. Megan had to admit he looked a lot better than the last time she'd seen him. His leg was still in a cast, but most of the other medical paraphernalia, including the beeping machines he'd been connected to in the hospital, were gone. He was wide awake and grinning.

"You came," he said, his brown eyes fixed on Megan. "I couldn't believe it when Mom said you called and were driving down from the Springs to see me."

"Mom and I were coming out of church when we decided." Megan hoped the reference to her mother would help put things in safer perspective.

Alex's gaze flitted from Megan to her mother. "I really appreciate it, Dr. Branson. Seriously. You don't know how boring it is just lying here all the time, watching TV and sleeping. I can't wait to get back to school and . . . " He paused, returning his eyes to Megan. "And back to a normal life again."

Megan's cheeks heated reheated, though she did her best to appear unfazed by his remarks. "So I understand from your mom that you can get up and walk around a bit now."

"A little. Not nearly enough, though. But at least I can eat regular food again."

"That's wonderful," Laura interjected. "Sounds as if you're well on the road to recovery."

Mrs. Williams responded before Alex could. "The doctor is really pleased with his progress." She smiled. "It'll be a while before he can go back to school, I'm sure, but at least he's out of the woods and we know he's going to be all right."

Megan knew her smile must appear strained, but she forced it anyway. Was he really going to be all right? Was she? And what was best for their baby? Did anything else really matter?

She was glad she still had a few weeks to make a final decision on her next move, and it was obvious she would have to spend a lot of that time in prayer.

※ ※ ※

LAURA DID HER BEST TO SHOVE THOUGHTS of Alex and Megan from her mind as she sat on the sofa with Jenny on Monday. They'd finished their clam chowder and were sipping cinnamon tea as the elderly woman prepared to reveal the next leg of Elizabeth Blackwell's journey.

The nearly finished quilt lay in her lap. "Are you ready?" She held up a corner of the quilt.

Laura nodded. The sooner they got into Dr. Blackwell's story, the sooner Laura could stop dwelling on her daughter and Alex—and their baby. At least, she hoped she could. She was certainly going to give it her best effort.

"All right, then. We left off during Elizabeth's educational years, her very difficult time at Geneva Medical School. She also worked during breaks from school, earning money for the many expenses she incurred as she studied. During one such extended break, she managed to land a position at Blockley Hospital and Almshouse, a hospital and shelter for the poorest of the poor. What she saw there was appalling. Though as a woman—and one who had yet to obtain a medical degree—she wasn't allowed to serve in any official medical capacity, she did receive permission to stay in the women's syphilitic wing, where she could study the patients. The things she saw and learned would have been enough to drive most prospective medical students into another field of endeavor, but not the woman who declared as a little girl that whatever she did when she grew up would be 'hard.' Little Shy persevered, living and working in deplorable conditions, and then returning to school to push on with her studies."

Laura shook her head. "I never cease to be amazed by her determination. I'm afraid I would have been one of those who threw in the towel long before that point. She must really have clung to her conviction that she was fulfilling God's purpose for her life."

"No doubt. How else would she have made it to that day at the end of January 1849, when she underwent the interrogation of a panel of professors and passed with flying colors? In fact, she graduated at the head of her class."

Laura smiled. She remembered that part in her long-ago studies of Elizabeth Blackwell. Hearing it this time, however, after realizing in detail the incredible obstacles the woman had overcome, warmed her heart in a way it never had before.

"Elizabeth even splurged and bought a new dress for the occasion, though it was a bit stiff and plain, to say the least—black with white lace trim—and her reddish hair was braided.

Her brother Henry, who was working relatively nearby, came for the occasion, which pleased her. Even the ladies of Geneva, who had ignored and turned away from Elizabeth, now came out in support of her, apparently thrilled to see one of their own gender reach such a monumental goal."

Laura nodded. "She made it. She got into medical school, and she graduated."

Jenny pointed to the next square on the quilt, one that looked much like the one she'd shown Laura when young Elizabeth and her family sailed from Europe to America.

"She had to sail the ocean again, didn't she?" Laura asked.

Jenny nodded. "You remember that part of her story, then."

"I do. But please tell it, will you?" She smiled, wanting to encourage her friend. "Somehow it means so much more when I hear it from you."

The older woman appeared pleased as she set the quilt back down on her lap. "All right, then. As you no doubt already know, dear Elizabeth had every bit as much trouble finding a place that would allow her to practice medicine as she did getting into medical school—maybe worse. She knew she had no hope of finding a position in America, and most of her doctor friends advised her to go to Paris, where she should have no difficulty. And so she set sail, landing in England on April 30, 1849. At the age of twenty-eight, Elizabeth returned to the land of her birth, a country she had left, along with her family, when she was a child of eleven. While there she visited many hospitals, but was still forced to go on to Paris in order to practice medicine. She spoke little French and had been warned about the great wickedness of Paris, but believing she could finally find a position there, she pressed on, as she always did. Sadly, however, she was met with the same resistance in Paris as she had everywhere else. No one, not even the liberal-minded Parisians, had much use for a woman physician."

"That's when she was forced to take a position at some sort of maternity hospital, wasn't it?"

Laura nodded. "Yes, I'm afraid so. *La Maternite*. It was the only place that would take her. And despite the fact that she'd graduated from medical college, she had to take an entry-level position with young, inexperienced novices who were training as midwives. It was a very difficult time, and as you probably already know, one that would change her life forever."

Laura nodded. The memory was vague and she would very much have liked to press Jenny to clarify it, but she glanced at her watch and knew she had to leave. "Same time tomorrow?" she asked as she stood and grabbed her coat from the arm of the sofa.

"I'll be looking forward to it."

❋ ❋ ❋

MEGAN SCUFFED THE TOE of her fleece-lined boot at a few remaining leaves as she crossed the campus toward her dorm room on Tuesday afternoon, nearly oblivious to the deepening cold and dark, heavy clouds overhead. It had been a mistake to visit Alex; she knew that now. By the time she and her mother had managed to get away Sunday afternoon, Alex seemed convinced they were once again an item.

"Call me when you get back to school," he said as the two women walked from his bedside toward the door of his room.

She turned back to look at him, telling herself he was only concerned with her welfare. But deep inside, she knew better. The proprietary tone she'd heard so many times during their relationship had returned. Ignoring her discomfort at that realization, she had simply nodded and agreed to do so.

Before she could turn back to follow her mother, who had now stepped outside the door into the hallway, he raised his hand and beckoned her to come to him. When she hesitated he chuckled, though she noticed he winced at the effort. "Please," he said, his voice scarcely above a whisper. "Can't you give me a kiss before you leave? Just one?"

Her heart had raced at the thought—whether in anticipation or at the audacity of his request, she wasn't sure, but she'd shaken her head no. "I have to go," was all she'd said, and the turned and hurried out the door, refusing to look back. Since then Alex had called her several times a day. Though she'd seldom answered, instead letting the calls go to voice mail, she was irritated with herself for allowing things to take such a negative turn.

Just like you did before, she reminded herself as her dorm came into sight. *How many times did you ignore the silent warnings to back off, to end the relationship before it turned into something destructive? But you didn't listen, and look what happened.*

Despite the fact she was outside, visible to the other students who crisscrossed the campus, she laid her hand over her stomach. She could blame Alex all day long for the situation she was in, but ultimately it was her fault, for she was the one who allowed it to happen.

Blinking away tears, she hurried up the porch and opened the door leading into the entryway. All she wanted was to lock herself in her room and have a good cry, but Lindy would probably be there, blasting her music, so crying was not an option.

She sighed as she climbed the stairs. It was only a couple more weeks until she headed home for the winter break, and she just hoped she could hold out until then.

Chapter 23

ALEX WAS GETTING AROUND A LITTLE BETTER each day, regaining strength and maneuvering his crutches well as he made his way from the bedroom to the rest of the house, particularly the kitchen. Since regaining his appetite he couldn't seem to get enough to eat, especially of his mom's great cooking.

That's one thing I sure don't miss about school, he thought as he traversed the hallway to the family room where he planned to watch some TV. He had a set in his room, but he was sick of lying in bed and wanted a change of scenery. *The cafeteria food on campus is terrible, but I'd put up with it if it meant spending time with Megan again.*

He lowered himself into the leather recliner where his dad usually sat when he was home from work. Pleased to have the comfortable chair to himself, he settled in and grabbed the remote. Daytime TV wasn't the best, but there should at least be some movies on that might not be too bad.

Browsing through them, he wondered what Megan was doing right now. He glanced at his watch. Ten thirty on Wednesday morning. No doubt she was in class. Was she thinking about him? He hoped so. After all, she'd come down to see him on Sunday, hadn't she? He just wished she'd been a little more affectionate, or that she'd call him more often now that she was back at school. His mom told him Megan had called to check on him daily while he was still in the hospital, but now that he was home and doing better, her phone calls had slowed to a trickle.

He sighed and picked a spy movie he'd seen before. The ending wouldn't be much of a surprise, but at least he knew it had a lot of action in it.

"Well, I see you're up and around. Feeling better today?"

He glanced up at the sound of his mom's voice. She stood in the doorway, smiling. Alex had to admit, she'd been faithful in watching over him after the accident, and he appreciated it.

"A little better every day." He returned her smile. "Must be all that TLC of yours—not to mention your cooking."

Mrs. Williams laughed. "No doubt. Speaking of which, are you hungry?"

"Getting there. Your breakfast was great, but that was a couple hours ago. I could go for a sandwich or something."

"Coming up."

She turned away, and he called after her. "Could you bring some chips and a soda with that?"

He heard her laugh again, and then he returned his attention to the movie. It would be perfect if Megan were sitting there beside him, but she wasn't, and he couldn't help wondering if she ever would be again.

Chloe. I'm always complaining that Megan doesn't return my phone calls, but I haven't exactly been good about returning Chloe's. He sighed and shook his head. *But why should I? She just wants to come down and see me, and what's the point? It's not like our relationship is going anywhere. The only thing we've got going on between us is physical, and I'm not really up to that yet. Maybe later . . . or maybe never.* He winced, ignoring the stab of guilt to his heart. *I'd really rather pick up where I left off with Megan. I just wish I knew if it was at least a possibility.*

He tilted the chair back to elevate his legs and thought again of Megan's last visit. It was as if she were giving him mixed messages. Why would she come if she didn't care? But if she still cared, why didn't she say so, or show it with a kiss or regular phone calls?

Women. No wonder men say they can't understand them.

"Here's your early lunch," his mother announced, entering the room and carrying a tray. She chuckled. "Though I imagine you'll be ready for another lunch before the afternoon is over."

"Count on it." Alex grinned. At least there was one woman in his life he could understand. His mom loved him and did everything she could to show it. Why couldn't Megan be more like her?

❄ ❄ ❄

LAURA HAD BEEN DISAPPOINTED when a flood of emergencies prevented her from breaking away to spend time with Jenny on Tuesday. It also reminded her of how much her routine had changed lately, as it hadn't been too long ago that she made a habit of working straight through lunch every day. But now it was Wednesday, and things were much slower at the clinic. She had breezed out for a lunch break without one pang of guilt. Jenny had surprised her by greeting her at the door of her shop, pleased to see her and eager to continue their story.

"Now let's see, where were we?" Jenny fingered the quilt as she squinted her eyes in concentration.

"We were talking about Elizabeth's time at *La Maternite* in Paris," Laura offered.

Jenny's face lit up. "Yes, of course. And as I said, it wasn't an easy time for her." She smiled. "But then, there weren't many easy times in Elizabeth's life, were there?"

Laura shook her head. "Apparently not."

"In fact," Jenny went on, once again lifting the quilt and this time pointing to a patch with an eye in the middle of it, "one of her most difficult times occurred during her fifth month at *La Maternite*. She was examining a baby with a serious eye infection. The light in the room was poor, so she leaned close to bathe his eyes—so close that some of the liquid squirted into her left one. She ignored it and continued working, despite the fact that her eye began to feel as if it had a grain of sand in it, and when she looked at it in the mirror, she noticed some swelling. The next morning when she awoke, she couldn't open that eye at all. The top and bottom lids were stuck together."

"How awful!" Laura shivered, remembering that she'd heard about this incident and its repercussions but hadn't paid much attention to it until now. "Remind me what happened as a result. I know she had recurring problems, didn't she?"

"She certainly did." Jenny set the quilt aside and continued. "In fact, she very nearly lost her sight entirely."

"Really?" Laura frowned. "Somehow I missed that part of her story. I remember it happened and caused her problems, but I hadn't realized how serious it was."

Jenny nodded. "Very serious indeed. Elizabeth went to her superiors and asked for time off to have the problem taken care of, but they told her she was overreacting and denied permission. Thankfully Elizabeth ignored them and went to the physician on duty, who immediately sent her to the infirmary. As it turned out her left eye was seriously infected, and the infection was beginning to spread to the right eye. The doctor informed the director, who had denied Elizabeth permission to have her eye examined and tended to, that he was removing her from duty and beginning treatment right away."

Knowing how primitive their medical methods were then compared to now, Laura asked, "What exactly did he do for her? I can imagine we would have all sorts of treatments for her today, most likely something as simple as antibiotics. But then?"

"You're right. They were severely limited at that time. The doctor cauterized her eyelids and attached leeches to her temples."

Laura felt a chill crawl up her spine. Leeches! A primary form of treatment for all sorts of ailments in those days, but hideous even to consider.

"They placed cold compresses on her eyes and covered her forehead with opium. For several days the doctor removed what he referred to as 'false membranes,' which continued to form over her eyes. But despite his excellent care, there was no real cure or treatment for her problem, and so everyone prayed and waited to see if Elizabeth would get better . . . or end up blind."

"What a tragedy that would have been." Laura considered the huge adjustment it would mean should such a thing happen to her. "As if her life wasn't difficult enough already!"

"How true. As it turned out, after a lengthy recovery period, the vision in her right eye was saved, but the damage to the left eye was beyond repair. She would have to continue her difficult journey with limited sight but renewed determination."

"Didn't she go to London from there?"

"For a time, yes. One of her cousins had managed to get her into St. Bartholomew's, one of the greatest hospitals in the city. She was quite excited and encouraged, as this meant she would receive official clinical training and would be able to make rounds to see all the female patients. She would even be able to see the male patients, except for the ones with syphilis. There were other perks as well, though she still wouldn't be accepted on an equal status with her male colleagues."

"But she went—half-blind and all."

"She went, yes, and was thrilled to do so. However, she first endured surgery to replace her damaged left eye with a glass one. Of course, her dream of eventually becoming a surgeon was now gone, but she simply made the adjustment to her dream and went on."

"Amazing." Laura could think of little else to say. "Absolutely amazing."

"Indeed. And so, in October 1850, Elizabeth left Paris behind and set out for London, ready to take on new challenges and build new dreams—which she did."

Laura smiled. "We have to stop for now, don't we?"

"Not on my account." Jenny laughed. "I could go on indefinitely, but I do believe you have a job waiting for you at the clinic."

"True." Laura picked up her purse from the floor beside her feet. "Same time tomorrow?"

"I certainly hope so. We're getting very close to Christmas, and I must hear from God about who is to receive this quilt. I also have a couple of squares to finish first, but I'm very nearly done." She pulled back the blue curtain and held it as Laura stepped out into the front room of the shop. "But we're making good progress with Elizabeth's story too, so I imagine it will all tie together at just the right time. God has a way of making that happen, doesn't He?"

Impulsively Laura put her arms around Jenny's shoulders in a quick embrace, then broke away and turned toward the front door. "It certainly seems that way." Silently she pleaded, *Please let it work out that way with Megan's situation, Lord. Please!*

※ ※ ※

BY WEDNESDAY EVENING Megan's nerves were stretched tight. She sat at her desk, hunched over her books, doing her best to drown out the noise that Lindy called music. How was she supposed to study in the middle of all this racket?

She sighed. Lindy was usually so good about restricting her music to earbuds, but occasionally she let it flood the room. Knowing what major problems some students had with their roommates, this seemed a small thing in comparison, so for the most part, Megan tried to ignore it and study anyway. But not tonight.

I give up. I may as well head for the library and try to study there. At least it'll be quiet.

She stood to her feet and gathered her books and papers together, then stuffed them into her backpack, along with her laptop. Slipping back into the parka she'd taken off a couple hours earlier, she headed for the door. As she reached for the doorknob, the music switched off.

"Where you going? I thought you said you were going to stay in and study."

Megan took a deep breath before turning around. She didn't want to blast the tall blonde who, for the most part, was a decent roommate, but she'd been holding too much inside for far too long.

"It's a little tough to concentrate in here," she said, keeping her voice low and even.

Lindy raised her perfectly shaped eyebrows and got up from her bed to face Megan. "Really? Why?"

Before Megan could answer, a look of understanding lit up the attractive young woman's face. "Ah, the music. Sorry about that. Why didn't you say something?"

Megan shrugged. "I didn't want to bother you about it."

Lindy laughed. "Bother me? Are you kidding?" She shook her head. "Megan, you are too much. Seriously! When are you going to learn to stick up for yourself? It's not like it would be an unreasonable request to ask me to keep my music down so you could study—or sleep, for that matter. Since you didn't say anything, I figured you didn't mind."

Megan felt her cheeks warm. Lindy was right. She really did need to be more pro-active and less passive about situations and issues that bothered her. Come to think of it, if she'd been less passive with Alex, she might not have gotten herself into such an awful situation with him.

"So," Lindy went on, recapturing Megan's attention, "I'll keep the music off or listen through my earbuds when you're studying or sleeping. Deal?"

Megan nodded, relieved. "Deal."

Lindy smiled, glancing at Megan's backpack. "That means starting tonight, so you don't have to leave the room to find somewhere to study. You were thinking about the library, weren't you? That place is way too cold and drafty. You do not want to go there on a night like tonight, girlfriend."

Megan stepped back toward her desk and set the backpack on the floor beside it. "Thanks. And you're right. I hate that cold library."

Lindy laughed. "Hey, speaking of cold, I could use a cup of hot chocolate. How about you? I've got at least two packages in my stash. We can pop two cups in the microwave, and they'll be ready in a couple minutes. A chocolate fix is always a good thing, right?"

Megan smiled. "Right. I never turn down chocolate."

Lindy busied herself with making the cocoa while Megan removed her books, papers, and laptop from her backpack and returned them to her desk. She cracked open a book and was ready to get started when Lindy set a steaming cup on the desk in front of her.

Megan looked up. "Thanks. I really appreciate this. Not just the hot chocolate, but . . . well, all of it."

Lindy nodded. "Like I said, you should have said something. I would have turned the music off or down, or just worn my earbuds." She shrugged. "I do that sometimes anyway, so it's not a problem. Really."

"Still, I appreciate your being so understanding. Maybe one of these days I'll learn to be a little more outspoken."

Lindy's blue eyes went serious. "Not a bad idea. Seriously, we've spent nearly a full semester together in this room, but we hardly know each other."

Megan knew that was true, but she enjoyed her privacy—especially now—and really didn't want to cross that line into intimate friendship.

Lindy grabbed the plain wooden chair in front of her own desk and pulled it over beside Megan's. "Now that we're on the subject, I have a question for you."

It was Megan's turn to raise her eyebrows as she waited.

"Are you . . . " Lindy paused and then asked, "are you pregnant?"

Megan felt her eyes widen as she struggled to take a deep breath. Where had that question come from? She hadn't said a word to anyone except her mother. Why would Lindy think such a thing?

"I caught you off-guard, didn't I?" Lindy laid a hand on Megan's arm. "Sorry. I didn't mean to, but . . . " She sighed. "Listen, I know it's none of my business, but I know the signs, OK?" She leaned closer. "Queasy in the morning, wanting to sleep a lot, that sort of thing. Been there, done that, all right? Twice. So not only do I know the signs, but I know what to do about it. And trust me, you don't want to wait. Get it taken care of early on, when it's not as big a deal."

Taken care of? Not a big deal? What was Lindy talking about?

The realization slammed her in the chest, and she nearly bent over as she felt the air exhale her lungs. An abortion? Lindy thought Megan should get an abortion?

Lindy frowned. "You're scared, aren't you? Listen, I don't blame you. I was too. But at least my boyfriend was around the first time to give me some support. He even paid for it. The second boyfriend was long gone before I could tell him about it, but that's OK. I didn't need him. I knew what to do by then, and I can help you." She paused. "It's that guy Alex, isn't it? He's the only one I've ever seen you with. But I thought you guys split up. You did, didn't you?"

Megan nodded, not trusting herself to speak.

"That's why I was so surprised when he came here right before Thanksgiving looking for you when you were visiting your mom." She frowned again. "Hey, didn't I hear he was in an accident or something? Is he OK? What happened?"

Megan nodded again, clearing her throat before trying to speak. "He . . . he was headed home for Thanksgiving too. I'm not sure of the details, but he ended up in the hospital with a broken leg, a few broken ribs, and a concussion. He's home now . . . with his parents, and he . . . he looks a lot better than he did. He's going to be all right, but it'll probably be a while before he can come back to school."

"Wow. I'm glad he's OK. But . . . how did you end up seeing him? If you two split up, why did you go to the hospital or his house? Are you guys getting back together?"

"No." Her answer shot out of her mouth before she could think about it. "I mean, we're still . . . friends. I care about him and want him to be OK, but that's it. Nothing more."

"Nothing? What about the pregnancy thing?" She tilted her head and studied Megan's face. "I just suspected before, but you didn't deny it, so now I know it's true. Does he know?"

"No. And I don't want him to—not yet anyway. I was going to tell him when we both got back to school after Thanksgiving, but I couldn't very well do it when he was lying in a hospital bed, or even after he got home. He's still healing and doesn't need any more pressure right now." She dropped her gaze. "Besides, I'm not even sure I want to tell him at all."

Lindy used a finger to tilt Megan's head back up. "Is it because of Chloe? I know they've been seeing each other since you and Alex broke up, but it doesn't seem very serious to me—at least not on Alex's part."

Megan shook her head. "Not really. The deal with Chloe just reinforces what I already thought about Alex. He's shallow and selfish and . . . immature. Not very good father material, you know?"

Lindy's laugh carried a trace of bitterness. "Are any of them? But seriously, why does it matter? You're not planning to go ahead with this thing, are you? Have the baby, I mean? Because if you're not, Alex never has to know." She shrugged. "I sure won't tell the big jerk. Why should I? Men are all the same. They just care about one thing—and it's sure not about what's best for us."

The thought flitted through Megan's head that Lindy's opinion of men just might be true, but then she pushed it away before it could take root. Megan's father had been a wonderful man, and she knew he wasn't the only one. She had just made a bad choice when it came to picking a boyfriend—and now she was paying the price.

Her baby would pay too, and that's what hurt her most. She knew she could never take Lindy's advice to "take care of the problem" by having an abortion. Her roommate meant well, but it was obvious their value systems were light years apart—though her current condition would make it nearly impossible to effectively convey her values to her roommate.

"Thanks for caring," she said, forcing a thin smile as she looked into Lindy's eyes. "But abortion is not an option for me. And right now, neither is telling Alex, so I really would appreciate your not saying anything—to him or anyone else. Please."

After a brief hesitation, Lindy nodded. "You see? You can be assertive when you want to be. Good for you!" She squeezed Megan's arm. "And don't worry. Your secret is safe with me. But remember, if you change your mind, I can help you make the arrangements."

"I won't change my mind."

"I know. You said that. But just in case."

Chapter 24

"ONE OF THE HIGHLIGHTS IN ELIZABETH'S STAY at St. Bartholomew's in London was meeting Florence Nightingale. They became quite good friends, actually." Jenny smiled as she delivered this news to Laura on Thursday during their lunch meeting in her back room.

Laura nodded. "I remember hearing they knew one another. What a friendship that must have been!"

"I should think so. Though Elizabeth became a doctor and Florence a nurse, both were pioneers in the medical field, and both overcame monumental obstacles and broke ground for many who were to follow behind them."

A feeling of gratitude and humility washed over Laura, as she was reminded again of how much she owed to those who had initially opened the doors so she and her female colleagues could one day step through them with relative ease.

Jenny sipped her lemon tea before continuing. "As you know, while Elizabeth labored first in France and then in London, her sister Emily had also opted to pursue a career in medicine and was actively seeking entrance into a medical school. Two medical schools for women had opened up during that time, so Emily's attempt wouldn't be nearly as difficult as Elizabeth's had been. And in the meantime, our beloved Little Shy, though pleased at what she had accomplished since leaving America, was desperately lonely for her family."

"I can imagine." Laura knew only too well what it was like to be separated from loved ones, though she couldn't get on a ship and sail across the ocean to reach Mitchell or Peter.

"Elizabeth had a hard time leaving the friends and supporters she'd made while in London, particularly Florence Nightingale who so shared her passion to bring healing to others. But on July 26, 1851, she boarded a ship bound for the United States and once again waved good-bye to the land of her birth."

"A difficult decision," Laura commented, "but one that led to her becoming the first woman doctor in America."

"Exactly." Jenny beamed. "And what an accomplishment that was!"

"I remember she met resistance even then."

"She certainly did. The first thing she did was walk the streets of New York, looking for a room to rent. Each time she'd see a sign, she'd knock on the door and introduce herself. When asked her profession, she honestly proclaimed herself a physician. Because of that, she had many doors slammed in her face. Part of the problem was that 'female physician' was the code name for abortionist in those days, making her quite unwelcome in most circles since few people knew of her firm pro-life stand."

"What did she do then?" Laura frowned. "I can't remember."

"She finally ended up renting an entire floor of rooms, spending half of her savings fixing up a bedroom and an office. But it was the only thing she could find. Then she hung out her shingle, as they say, and waited for patients to show up."

Laura laughed. "I'm sorry. I know it's not funny, but I'm picturing this poor woman who has worked so hard and come so far, now reduced to spending more money than she can afford, hanging out her sign in hopes of a response, and then sitting with hands folded, waiting."

"Perhaps those hands were folded in prayer."

Laura raised her eyebrows. "I hadn't thought of that, but you may very well be right."

"I would think so. How else would she persevere in the face of such adversity?"

How indeed? Laura had no other answer.

"In the meantime, though she too had met with much resistance, Elizabeth's sister Emily, who longed to follow in her sister's footsteps, managed to gain admittance to Rush Medical College in Chicago. And Elizabeth, since she still had no patients, decided to lecture about women's health issues. Many of her talks were published, helping to spread her notoriety. This writing and speaking garnered her a bit of income and even some support of her right to practice medicine. Some of those who heard her speak, particularly Quakers, became her first patients. At last Dr. Blackwell was establishing her practice."

Laura smiled. It seemed a good place to break and return to work, though she knew she'd be back for more the next day.

❈ ❈ ❈

"YOU HAVE COMPANY."

His mother's voice worked its way into Alex's sleep, and he stirred, opening his eyes slowly to focus on the familiar face standing over him at his bedside.

"Megan?" Her name came out before he could think of anyone else. Was it possible she'd come back to see him? But it was only Friday. Had she taken off early from school again?

His mother's smile faded. "No, sweetheart. It's not Megan. It's Pastor Stafford. Remember I told you last night that he said he'd drop by this morning?"

Alex's heart deflated, but he forced a smile. "Sure, Mom. I remember."

"Would you like me to ask him to wait so you can come out and talk with him in the family room, or do you want him to come in here?"

Alex considered the effort it took to get up and make it into the other room. Admittedly he did it a couple times a day now, but why bother when the pastor could just as easily come to him? After all, pastors and doctors were used to sitting at bedsides.

"If you'll just get me an extra pillow, I'll sit up right here."

Mrs. Williams nodded. "Of course. There's one right here."

In moments she had retrieved a pillow from a nearby chair and placed it behind his back. He scooted up and settled in enough that he was ready for a visit. "Have him come on in."

She leaned down and kissed his forehead. "How about if I bring in some hot tea? Or would you prefer iced?"

"Either is fine, Mom. Really."

She nodded and exited the room, leaving the door open. Almost immediately Pastor Stafford stepped through it.

"Hey, Alex," he said, smiling as he walked toward the bed, hand extended.

Alex took it, and they shook briefly before the pastor sat down in the chair beside the bed.

"So how are you doing? You're looking much better, and your mom says you're getting up and moving around the house a bit now." He chuckled. "She says she knows you're getting better because you're back to eating them out of house and home again."

Alex smiled. "She's right about that. Seems like I'm hungry all the time."

"Nothing wrong with that. You've come a long way in a short time, you know. We weren't sure if you'd make it at first, so it's great to see your improvement. And if we have to rival the national debt to keep you fed, we'll all pitch in and do it."

Alex appreciated the pastor's levity, but he also appreciated his obvious concern. Next to his parents, Pastor Stafford had spent more time at his bedside right after the accident than anyone else. Alex had always liked the pastor, and he knew his mom and dad thought very highly of him.

"So what's next? I imagine you're anxious to get back to school."

Yes and no, Alex wanted to say. *I don't want to get back to my studies, but I do want to get back to Megan.* But of course he wasn't about to say that. "You're right, but realistically I doubt I'll be up to it until after the winter break, so that's what I'm shooting for."

"Must be tough to get so far behind on your studies."

I was already behind. This just gives me a convenient excuse so my dad won't stop paying my tuition and make me get a job. Once again, he kept his thoughts to himself. "It's going to take a lot of work to catch up once I'm back, but I'm going to work hard at making it happen."

The pastor nodded. "Hard work and determination are good things." He smiled. "Sometimes not enough, though."

Alex frowned. "I don't understand."

"I'm not talking about schoolwork or studies, or even jobs and professions. I'm talking about having a real relationship with God. We can never work hard enough to make that happen, you know."

Uh-oh. Here it came. The old "salvation pitch." He should have known. After all, he'd heard it at church and in Sunday School, and even from his parents, countless times over the years. And maybe there was something to it, something more than just making an appearance in church now and then and praying when you were in trouble. But even so, Alex just wasn't ready. He was young, with his whole life ahead of him. He wasn't about to stop having fun and start living like a monk. But how could he say that to Pastor Stafford without being rude?

"Tea's ready!" His mother's voice at the door gave him just the out he needed. He smiled widely as she came in, balancing a tray with a pot of tea, two cups, sliced lemons, creamer and sugar, and a small stack of cookies.

"Thanks, Mom," he said. She had no idea how much he meant it.

※ ※ ※

JENNY WAS PLEASED to continue with Elizabeth's story that Friday at noon, but she sensed it was growing ever more important to Laura. The older woman had risen early that morning, wrapping herself in her warm robe and carrying her Bible to her favorite chair in her bedroom. There she had conversed with God for more than an hour, much of the time spent on Laura and Megan. Though Jenny still didn't know any specifics about why she prayed for the two women, she sensed an urgency to continue.

"Didn't Dr. Blackwell eventually start a clinic in one of the poorest sections of New York?"

Laura's question hit at the heart of what Jenny had been thinking about as she told the story of Elizabeth Blackwell. "She did, and not long after she began to have some success with her writing and lecturing. It was in March 1853, when she opened a dispensary for those who had absolutely no means to pay her, announcing that she would see patients free of charge three afternoons a week. The dispensary was located on Tompkins Square, right in the middle of the tenements of the Eleventh Ward, when pigs still ran in the streets—and so did blood. It was a filthy, dangerous area, but the need for medical attention was nearly as great as Elizabeth's heart to serve. Area residents were suspicious of her, to say the least, but desperation drove them to her. By January of the following year, Elizabeth had become so successful in this particular venture that she was able to incorporate the New York Dispensary for Poor Women and Children."

Laura's smile lit up her face. "A woman after my own heart."

"She certainly was," Jenny agreed. "Or is it the other way around? With your work at the clinic, I imagine she would consider you a woman after her heart."

Laura nodded. "Yes, that would be more accurate, wouldn't it?"

"And it wasn't just her free clinic that grew. Her private practice was taking off too. In fact, it wasn't long before a German immigrant named Marie Zakrzewska, a professional midwife with training at the medical college at the University of Berlin, joined Elizabeth. Zak, as she came to be known, quickly improved her English and studied under Elizabeth until Elizabeth was able to get Zak admitted to medical school in Cleveland. Zak promised to return and work with Elizabeth when her two years of study were over."

Jenny took the last sip of her tea and smiled at Laura, praying her words were encouraging her somehow. "Elizabeth's heart soared at the thought of having Zak as a partner. She was already dreaming of the day when her sister would complete medical school and become part of her practice. Now it seemed God had provided for a threesome of women physicians to carry the dream forward."

"Beautiful." Laura smiled, and Jenny noted a hint of tears in her eyes. "Absolutely beautiful. Hearing this story from you is like hearing it for the first time. Thank you, my friend."

"It's my pleasure. Truly it is."

Chapter 25

THE MOUNTAIN TOWERED ABOVE HIM, so tall he couldn't see the top. He reached out his hand to touch it, but quickly withdrew. Its sides were like dry ice—cold and yet burning at the same time. How was he ever to scale such a monstrosity? And yet scale it he must. That much was obvious. The mountain blocked every effort at any other forward progress. There was no way around it or under it, so climbing it was the only solution. And yet it was impossible.

Climbing gear. That's what I need. Though he'd never climbed a mountain in his life, he decided he needed picks and axes and rope. Surely then he could get over the top.

He glanced to his side, where the gear he wanted suddenly appeared, lying on the ground beside him. Hopeful, he looped the rope over his shoulder and tried to figure out a way to carry the rest of the equipment while climbing. Once again, he sensed he was facing the impossible. Still, he had to try.

Slipping on the heavy gloves that had appeared with the other equipment, he tried to get a handhold on the mountain, even as he struggled to dig the toes of his boots into the tiny crevasses that pocked the monolith. He was sweating and panting for breath in a matter of minutes, though he'd progressed only a couple of inches upward.

Spotting a tree branch sticking out from the rocky mass, he reached up and grabbed it, hoping to pull himself upward and gain some ground. He'd no sooner clutched the branch than it gave way and he tumbled back down to the ground where he had started. Determined to persevere, he jumped to his feet and tackled the mountain again, this time climbing a few inches higher than the first time before he fell. Now he lay in a heap at the foot of the mountain, crying in frustration.

"Will you let Me help you?"

The voice, warm and smooth as honey, flowed over him, calling him back from his despair. Confused yet hopeful, he lifted his eyes toward the source of the voice. The glare of sunlight kept him from discerning the Man's face, but His outstretched hand was close enough to touch. In the center of it was a scar, as if something had been pounded through it.

"I know You," he whispered, fear and awe intertwined in his pounding heart. "I know You!"

"Yes," came the answer. "You know Me in your head. But to know Me in your heart, you must admit your need and take My hand. Are you ready at last to let Me carry you?"

He swallowed. "Will You . . . carry me over that mountain?"

"I will. There's no other way to the other side, you know."

He nodded. Somehow he knew the Man spoke the Truth, and he wanted desperately to accept His offer. But what if . . . what if the Man found out what he had done and rejected him? Then what?

"Alex? Alex, wake up, sweetheart."

The woman's voice came from far away, calling him back from the mountain and the Man with the outstretched hand. He wrestled between the two worlds until finally he yielded to his mother's voice and opened his eyes.

She stood beside his bed, gazing down at him. "I'm sorry to wake you, but I need to make a quick run to the store. I won't be long, but I didn't want you waking up and wondering where I was. I'll make your breakfast as soon as I get back. Will you be OK while I'm gone?"

Alex blinked in an attempt to clear his mind. He knew he'd been dreaming, but it seemed so real.

His mother was waiting for an answer. He took a deep breath. "Sure, Mom. Go ahead. I'll be fine."

She smiled and patted his shoulder. "I'll be back before you know it. I promise."

Alex nodded. "No problem. I'll be right here."

He watched her walk from the room, alarm rising in his chest at the thought of being alone. Why? What was he afraid of? He was safe and sound in the home where he'd grown up. He was healing from his wounds. His mom would be back within the hour.

Wait a minute. It's Saturday. Where's Dad? He's not working today.

Then he remembered. His father had mentioned last night that he had a meeting at church early this morning.

Church. Pastor Stafford. I wonder if he'd come over if I called him.

He knew then why he felt a sense of alarm. It was the dream. The memories came flooding back, and he shivered in spite of the pile of covers on top of him. Yes, he really needed to talk to someone about the dream, and Pastor Stafford seemed the most obvious person.

※　※　※

LINDY HAD KEPT HER WORD about using her ear-buds to listen to her music, leaving Megan with no obvious excuse for not studying—or for going home for the weekend again.

It was Saturday morning, and the temptation to jump in her car and head south to the Springs had been dancing around in her head since the night before. Quite obviously she could no longer say, as she had the previous weekend, that she needed a quiet place to study, so why the pull to escape the campus again? She couldn't decide if the main attraction was her familiar room at home, time with her mother, listening to Mrs. Townsend's stories about Elizabeth Blackwell . . . or Alex. Though her mind insisted she wanted nothing to do with the man who was the father of her unborn child, her heart still nudged in his direction from time to time. And this was one of those times.

"Want to head over to the coffee shop and pick up a couple of iced coffees and some donuts? I noticed you didn't get down to the cafeteria in time for breakfast either. I'm starting to get hungry, aren't you?"

Megan raised her eyes from the open book on her desk and turned to look at her roommate. The attractive blonde sat cross-legged on her bed, where she did much more of her studying than at her desk. She still wore her earbuds, though she'd pulled one from her ear, enabling Megan to hear the music that seemed to be Lindy's constant companion.

"I'm really not all that hungry," Megan said, though her stomach was beginning to feel a bit empty. "I thought I'd just study until noon or so and then go to the cafeteria for lunch."

Lindy shrugged. "Suit yourself. I've got an irresistible urge for sweet, so I'm going, with or without you. You want me to bring you something?"

Megan considered it, then shook her head. "No, I'm fine. Thanks."

Lindy rose from the bed and crossed the room toward Megan. "You're not still having morning sickness, are you?"

Megan hated the telltale flush that crept up her neck and into her face, but not as much as she hated the fact that

Lindy knew her secret. "I'm . . . over it, yes. Pretty much, anyway. That's not why I don't want to eat yet. I'm just not hungry. But thanks for asking."

Lindy shrugged again. "Morning sickness or not, you'd better do something about your problem soon, before you start showing. You can't hide it forever, you know, and it's a lot harder to get rid of if you wait."

Get rid of. The words sliced through Megan's gut with searing heat. She knew Lindy wasn't purposely trying to hurt her. She also knew that her roommate saw absolutely nothing wrong with ending a life, so long as that life was still tucked away in someone's womb. But Megan was sickened by the words. Though having a child at this stage of her life was certainly not something she'd planned, that didn't change the fact that she had no intention of doing away with the developing baby inside her.

"I'm . . . not having an abortion," she said, looking straight into Lindy's eyes. "I'm not sure what I'm going to do, but abortion is not an option."

Lindy stared at Megan for several seconds before breaking away and turning back toward her bed. "Whatever," she said, grabbing her jacket and slipping it on. "Anyway, I'm heading out. Last chance to change your mind."

Megan shook her head. "I'll wait for lunch, thanks."

Lindy grabbed the large silver-colored bag she carried everywhere and slung it over her shoulder. "All right, then. Guess we'll be locked in here together all weekend, studying. See you in a while."

When the door shut behind her, Megan closed the book that lay on the desk in front of her. She may not have had an excuse to go home before this, but now she did. The last thing in the world she wanted was to spend the weekend locked away in her small room with the only person besides her mother who knew about the baby—and who thought she should kill it and get on with her life.

Tossing things into her backpack and small roller suitcase, she decided she'd call her mom on the way. Above all, she wanted to be gone before Lindy returned.

❉ ❉ ❉

Megan rolled into town just before noon, and by now her stomach was growling. She'd called her mom and agreed to meet her at Jenny's Treasures for lunch. Her mother had assured her they had plenty so she didn't need to stop and pick up anything.

The sun, though thin, perched unencumbered in a cloudless sky as Megan parked her car and headed toward the shop. Her mother's car was already there, directly in front of the entrance.

Megan stepped inside, welcomed by the familiar tinkling bells that hung on the door. Her mother and Jenny stood at the counter in front of the blue curtain, chatting. Their heads turned in unison when she entered.

"You made it," Laura exclaimed, hurrying toward her for a hug.

Jenny was right behind. "What a lovely surprise! I was so pleased when your mother said you were joining us."

Megan smiled as she flipped the sign to Closed and locked the door. "It was a last-minute decision, but I figured the weather was good and it's only an hour drive, so why not?"

"Why not indeed?" Jenny agreed, leading the way to the back room.

Laura walked beside Megan, leaning toward her to ask, "Is everything all right?"

Megan raised her eyebrows. "Sure. Everything's fine. Why wouldn't it be?" But even as she asked the question, she knew why her mother was concerned. She smiled and kissed her mother's cheek. "Really, Mom. Everything's fine. I just wanted to come home for the weekend."

"I'm glad you did." Laura returned her daughter's smile. "I just worry about you sometimes."

Megan laughed. "No kidding. You always used to tell me that's part of your job description, remember?"

They stepped behind the curtain and settled in on the couch. Apparently Laura had already placed their lunch on the coffee table before Megan arrived because a large, flat white box, with the words *Tony's Pizzas* on the top, sat waiting for them.

"It smells wonderful," Megan exclaimed, realizing she hadn't had a pizza in quite a while. "What kind is it?"

"Half pepperoni and olives," Laura answered, "and half everything."

Megan's mouth watered as they scooped pieces onto paper plates and Mrs. Townsend offered a blessing before they took their first taste. Megan took a slice from each half of the pizza, and she wasn't disappointed as she took a bite of each. Both were every bit as delicious as she'd anticipated.

They talked and laughed between bites until they all exclaimed they were stuffed and couldn't eat anymore. Then, at last, Jenny Townsend picked up her quilt from the arm of the sofa and placed it in her lap.

"I'm nearly done with this," she said, smiling at her two guests. "I must pass this gift on to its intended recipient as soon as the Lord reveals to me who that may be. So I think it's appropriate that you're both here today to hear me wrap up this story of Elizabeth 'Little Shy' Blackwell."

Megan felt her eyes widen in surprise. "You're almost done with the story? Did I really miss that much while I was gone this week?"

"Don't worry," Laura said, laying her hand on Megan's arm. "I'll fill you in before you go back to school tomorrow."

Jenny nodded. "Very good. And again, as I said, it's appropriate, Megan, that you're here for this part of the story, though it will be a quick summary of the last part of her life, I'm afraid. Still, I want to stress that Elizabeth's loneliness was no doubt the impetus for something she did in October 1854. She went to an orphanage and picked out a child— a girl of about seven or eight named Kitty—and adopted her. Strangely enough, the girl always referred to Elizabeth as 'my doctor,' but the two of them became quite close over the years."

"I don't remember that part of the story at all," Megan said. "That says a lot about Dr. Blackwell, doesn't it? She didn't have a husband and spent so much time away from her mother and siblings. No wonder she felt the need for some-one to spend time with . . . to love and who would love her."

From the corner of her eye, Megan saw her mother turn her head and gaze at her before returning her attention to Jenny. Together they waited for the story to continue.

"By 1856 some of Elizabeth's family had moved to New York. In addition, Zak and Emily had joined the practice, so it seemed things were falling into place for Elizabeth at last. She so wanted to establish a hospital, staffed by women, and on May 12, 1857—Florence Nightingale's birthday, by the way—Elizabeth and her partners, Zak and Emily, did exactly that. They officially opened the New York Infirmary for Indigent Women and Children. It was a great success. Though there were still many hurdles to overcome, they were on their way, though Zak eventually moved on. By 1860, Elizabeth and Emily decided they needed to open a medical school for women."

Laura frowned. "I don't remember that they actually did that—at least not then. Am I wrong?"

Jenny smiled. "Plans were well underway and finances being sought when everything changed. It was April 1861, and I'm sure you know what happened then."

Megan spoke up immediately. "The Civil War."

Jenny nodded. "Exactly. The next thing they knew they were knee-deep in training nurses to tend to the thousands of wounded. It was a major turning point in the previously male-dominated nursing profession. The need was so great, and women rushed to fill that need. And, of course, throughout the war Elizabeth became even more vocal and active in her longstanding crusade against slavery."

Laura spoke up then. "It was just a few years after the war that Elizabeth was finally able to establish that medical school for women, right?" She nodded as she spoke. "It's coming back to me now."

"Exactly," Jenny said. "It was November 1868, to be exact, when the Women's Medical College of the New York Infirmary officially opened its doors. Another of Elizabeth's dreams had been realized."

"And what a price she paid over the years," Megan commented.

Jenny smiled. "We seldom see our dreams come true without paying a heavy price, do we?"

Megan knew the elderly woman was right. Instinctively she placed her hand on her stomach.

"Elizabeth had accomplished what she'd set out to do, but she was tired." Jenny took another sip of tea before continuing. "On July 15, 1869, with the infirmary and college established and able to run without her, she climbed aboard a ship and left America behind, returning to the land of her birth."

Laura nodded. "Yes, I remember that she went back to England."

"She certainly did." Jenny set her cup down. "Of course, she didn't rest on her laurels there either. She set up a medical practice in London and taught at the London School of Medicine for Women—which she helped establish, by the way—but she was too frail and weary to continue for long.

In March 1879 she and Kitty moved to a charming country house where she spent her last years writing articles, lectures, and books. It was a fitting way to pass on much of what she'd learned to those who would come along after her."

"Like us," Megan said, glancing at her mother, who nodded.

"She made it until May 31, 1910, when she left this world and went at last to be with her Savior. No doubt she heard Him speak those wonderful words, 'Well done, good and faithful servant.'"

Well done. Yes, those were the words Megan wanted spoken about her when she passed on. But she knew that would only happen if, like Dr. Blackwell, she set herself to fulfill God's purpose, regardless of the cost.

Chapter 26

"THAT'S QUITE A DREAM." Pastor Stafford looked serious as he sat beside Alex's bed. "Have you ever had a similar one before?"

Alex shook his head. "Not really. I mean, things like I couldn't run when I wanted to or couldn't talk or something. But this was different."

The pastor nodded. "It sounds that way. Do you have any thoughts about what it might mean? Quite obviously you feel it's more than just your run-of-the-mill dream or you wouldn't have called me."

Alex had second-guessed his decision to call Pastor Stafford ever since he'd hung up the phone. He'd even considered calling back and telling him not to bother coming over after all. But deep down he knew the dream would haunt him until he talked to someone about it. He was just glad the pastor had been available and willing to come over, and that his parents had honored Alex's request to let him talk with the pastor alone.

"I keep telling myself there's nothing to it. It's just a dream, period." He shrugged, though quickly regretted the movement as a pain shot through his still-healing ribs. "I . . . I guess I know it really does mean something, but I can't figure out what."

Pastor Stafford's smile was gentle, as was his touch as he laid his hand on Alex's arm. "Alex, you've been raised in church. You've heard the gospel countless times, but the truth is, you've never really grasped its message." He paused. "And you've never truly received Jesus as your Savior, have you?"

Alex resisted the impulse to tell the man he was wrong. After all, he believed in Jesus . . . didn't he? He knew Jesus was the Son of God and that He'd died on the Cross. Wasn't that enough? He'd heard countless times about the need to receive Jesus as his Savior, but he assumed that had happened somewhere along the line . . . hadn't it?

At that moment, he somehow knew it hadn't. But what was he supposed to do about it? And what did the dream have to do with any of this?

"I've always known about Jesus being the Savior," Alex said. "I mean, I heard about it from my parents and at church practically from day one. But now, all of a sudden, I'm not so sure."

Pastor nodded. "And that's the point. Knowing that Jesus is the Savior isn't enough. That's just accepting a fact in your mind." He paused. "It isn't until you actually meet Jesus—face-to-face, heart-to-heart—that you understand how absolutely lost you are without Him. He's your only hope, Alex. When Jesus said, 'I am the way and the truth and the life; no one comes to the Father except through Me,' He meant it. There is absolutely, positively no other way to God except through His Son, Jesus Christ. I know that flies in the face of today's tolerant, 'anything goes' society, which declares that all belief systems are equal and no one has the right to impose his or her standards on someone else. But the fact is, saying that Jesus Christ is the only way to get to God isn't imposing our standards on anyone. It's simply telling others what God Himself has said."

Alex's mind was reeling. What was the pastor saying? No other way? Only Jesus? What about Buddhists and Hindus and Muslims—and even atheists? Were they all wrong in their beliefs?

"Do you remember that mountain you saw in your dream?" Pastor asked.

Did he remember? If he could have blocked it out of his thoughts, the two of them wouldn't be having this discussion right now. He nodded but said nothing.

"I believe that mountain may have represented your inability to reach God by your own efforts. Getting to God on your own is even more of a challenge than climbing that mountain. In fact, it's impossible. And you want to know why?"

Alex wished he didn't have to know but he realized he must. He nodded.

"Because every single one of us has sinned, and God cannot allow sin into His presence. You couldn't climb the mountain in your dream in the same way you can't overcome your own sin in order to have a relationship with God. It simply can't be done. But nearly everyone who's ever lived tries to find a way to do it. When they realize they can't make it on their own, their choices are limited. They can join some religion and try to follow the rules closely enough that they dare to hope God will let them into Heaven when they die, or they can give up entirely and try to convince themselves that God doesn't exist. Of course, they can also choose the truth, which is that Jesus is the only way to get to God and that He's just waiting for us to come and ask Him."

Tears pricked Alex's eyes, and he blinked them away, embarrassed. He hated anything that made him feel weak, and right now that's exactly how he felt.

"That's what it means for Jesus to be your Savior. It's not just acknowledging that the church calls Him the Savior; it's coming to Him and acknowledging that you're a sinner with absolutely no way to mend the broken relationship between yourself and God. Jesus didn't just die on the Cross for the sins of the world, Alex, though He did do that. But He also died for your sins—and for mine. Because of what He did, all we have to do is receive His forgiveness, and He automatically restores us to a relationship with His Father."

Pastor Stafford paused again, and Alex knew he should say something, but he just didn't trust himself to do so. Instead he waited.

"Are you ready to do that, Alex? To receive God's forgiveness and to truly know Jesus as Savior—face-to-face and heart-to-heart?"

Alex's thoughts and emotions tumbled inside him, as he realized the obvious: that the Man in his dream was Jesus, and the pastor's words just mirrored what God was already speaking to his heart. He nodded, as the first tears spilled from his eyes and ran down his face.

"Good. I'll pray, and you can repeat after me. Can you do that?"

Alex nodded again.

"Dear Lord," the pastor prayed, "I know I'm a sinner and my sins stand between us."

Speaking barely above a whisper, Alex repeated the words, the truth of them clutching his heart.

"I also know Jesus paid the price for those sins when He hung on the cross."

Once again, Alex repeated the words.

"I ask You to forgive me, Lord. I want Jesus to be my Savior, and I want to have a relationship with You."

Alex stumbled over the first few words, realizing at that exact moment how very much he needed God's forgiveness. But then he took a deep breath and continued before waiting for the pastor's next words. When they came he thought they were the most wonderful words he'd ever heard.
"Thank You, Father, for making me Your child forever."

Alex finished the prayer with his own words: "I don't really understand all this yet, God, but I'm ready to learn. I want to change. I want to be the man You want me to be. Please help me." He buried his face in his hands then, sobbing as an incredible sense of joy washed over him. For the first time He knew without doubt that God was real, that Jesus was His Son, and that he, Alex Williams, now had a relationship with God that nothing or no one could ever sever.

* * *

LAURA WASN'T SURPRISED when Megan invited her to come along after church the next day for a brief visit to check on Alex. She told herself that Megan's concern was due in part to her caring nature, as well as the fact that Alex was the baby's father—even if he didn't know anything about it. But in spite of her reassurances, Laura was still uncomfortable with the entire situation.

Why? The question echoed in her mind as they barreled down the highway toward Pueblo. The sky was clear and the wind calm, so Laura hadn't argued when Megan insisted on driving her own car.

"It's so much cheaper on gas," she'd argued.

Laura knew that was true, but she hated the tiny vehicle anyway. She imagined her feelings for the minicar were about the only thing she and Alex had in common.

Back to Alex, she thought. And back to the question of why Megan bothered to go see him when she could simply call his mother to confirm that he was doing well and then go on with her life. Quite obviously her daughter still cared for Alex Williams, though Laura couldn't for the life of her imagine why.

I can't figure out what she saw in him in the first place, she thought as they pulled off the freeway and headed toward the Williamses' home. *But I suppose she recognized some positive traits in him that I just haven't discovered yet.*

Megan seemed pleasantly surprised when Alex greeted them at the door—on crutches, but at least getting around on his own.

"You look great," Megan announced when Alex answered the door. "You're really getting around great."

Her cheeks flushed the moment she said the words, and Laura couldn't help but wonder if her daughter was embarrassed at having implied more in her comment than the obvious surprise she'd felt at seeing him up and around.

"Thanks." Alex grinned at Megan, obviously pleased, and the girl quickly averted her eyes. "I was really glad when you called and said you were coming."

Mrs. Williams popped in then, saving the day with her presence. "It's so nice to see you both again. Come in, please. Where would you all like to sit? Since Alex is getting around so well, we can visit in the kitchen or the family room . . . whatever you prefer." She glanced at Alex as if waiting for him to make the call.

"I'd like to talk to Megan privately." He cut his eyes from Megan to Laura to his mother, and then back to Megan. "Just for a little while," he added, still gazing at Megan. "Please."

Megan hesitated before nodding, and Mrs. Williams picked up the conversation as if on cue, taking Laura by the arm. "This is perfect," she said, escorting Laura toward the kitchen. "It will give us a few minutes to get to know one another better while I fix some tea." She peered up at Laura. "I assume you two had lunch on the way down?"

Laura confirmed that they had, and Mrs. Williams smiled. "All right, then. You and I will slice some pound cake and we can have dessert with our tea."

They were standing inside the Williamses' warm, yellow-toned kitchen by then, and Laura felt herself relax a bit despite her concern over Alex and Megan being alone. Where would the conversation go? Would Megan hold strong in her commitment to keep the news of the baby private for the time being?

"I'll put the kettle on, and you can slice the cake. Let me get you a proper knife."

Mrs. Williams's voice cut into Laura's fretting, and she pulled herself back to the very pleasant lady who stood in front of an open drawer, fumbling for just the right utensil. "Here you go," she announced, pulling out a silver cake server and handing it to her.

Laura smiled and took it from her. "This is lovely. Thank you."

Mrs. Williams smiled as she filled the kettle and put it on the stove. "It's was my grandmother's. It's one of the few things I still have of hers, and I love using it."

"I know what you mean." Laura stepped up to the counter where Mrs. Williams had placed a cutting board and the pound cake. "I have only a few family heirlooms, but they're among my most prized possessions."

Mrs. Williams nodded as she pulled down four cups and saucers from the cupboard. "Isn't it funny how little most of our material possessions matter to us, especially as we get older? Unless, of course, there's a personal or sentimental meaning behind them."

The two women continued to chat as they set the table, and Laura found herself needing to excuse herself to use the restroom. Mrs. Williams pointed her down the hallway toward the second door on the right. Laura had just grabbed the door handle when she heard her daughter's voice coming from the next room. Laura stiffened when she realized Megan was crying.

"I want to forgive you," she was saying between sobs, "but you . . . you forced me, Alex. Some people would even say you raped me. At the same time, I . . . I know I should have set boundaries long before we got to that point. Maybe if I had, none of the rest of this would . . . would ever have happened."

Laura heard Alex groan. "Oh Megan, I'm so sorry. I really am. I told myself you wanted it as much as I did, and somehow that made it all right in my mind. But now I . . . I know it wasn't. There was nothing right about it at all."

Soundlessly, Laura let herself into the bathroom and closed the door behind her. She couldn't bear to hear another word. *Alex had raped Megan?* The thought nearly knocked Laura to her knees. Why hadn't Megan told her? This changed everything—absolutely everything. Why didn't Megan seem to realize that? Once again, the option of abortion, which Laura had refused to acknowledge, danced dangerously close to her conscious thoughts.

❅ ❅ ❅

IT HAD TAKEN EVERY OUNCE OF RESTRAINT Laura could muster to get through the remainder of their visit and then the ride home, but she'd been determined not to bring up what she'd heard until she'd had time to digest it. She just wished Megan would open the conversation by divulging what had happened so Laura wouldn't have to broach it at all. But since Megan hadn't chosen to do that yet, Laura questioned if she ever would. It was obviously just too personal and painful for her to put into words.

But now Laura was home once again, having kissed her daughter and watched her drive off on her way back to school. How would she ever keep this to herself?

I can pray, she reminded herself. *And that had better be my first choice. But Lord, You know I need someone else to talk with too—someone "with skin on," as the saying goes.*

Jenny. Of course! Did she dare tell her what was going on? It wasn't that Laura didn't trust the dear woman, for there wasn't a doubt in Laura's mind that Jenny would keep the situation to herself. But Laura couldn't help but wonder how the elderly woman would deal with such information.

There's only one way to find out.

She glanced at her watch. It was nearly five. Surely Jenny hadn't gone to bed yet, but might she be getting ready to go back to church for the evening service, assuming her church had one?

I should wait until tomorrow. We've finished Dr. Blackwell's story, but I'm sure she wouldn't mind my coming by for lunch anyway.

Laura tried to push the topic from her mind, telling herself she needed to make a light supper and spend some time reading her Bible and praying, but all she could think about were the words she'd heard spoken between her daughter and Alex.

He raped her. He raped her! Oh God, how am I going to let go of this? Tears bit her eyes and refused to be blinked away. *I'm angry, Father. I'm really, really angry.*

Jenny's wise face danced in and out of her mind. "That's it," she said aloud. "I'm going to give her a call. If she's not home or not up for company, fine. But I'm going to try."

Jenny answered on the first ring, as if she'd been waiting for her, and she didn't sound in the least surprised by Laura's request. "Why, of course you can come over. I hadn't planned on doing anything special this evening, and I'd love the company."

The next thing Laura knew, she was pulling up in front of her friend's house, carrying a bag with two containers of steaming hot chili, picked up at the deli along the way. Sharing a meal while they talked had become a habit with the two women, and Laura saw no reason to change it now.

"Chili!" Jenny's blue eyes sparkled as she welcomed Laura into her home. "One of my favorites. Let's take it straight into the kitchen, shall we? I have hot cider on the stove. I thought you might like a change from tea."

"Either is fine, but yes, cider sounds wonderful. I just hope the chili isn't too spicy for you."

Jenny chuckled. "Even if it is, I'll gladly eat an antacid or two for dessert."

In moments they were settled around the table, enjoying their chili and cider, while Laura talked about Megan's weekend visit, laying the groundwork for the direction she really wanted to go with their conversation.

"I'm sure you're enjoying all these weekend visits from your daughter," Jenny commented as she refilled their cups. "But she hasn't always come home on the weekends since she's been in college, has she?"

Laura shook her head. "No. Just lately. She . . . " Was this the time? *Oh Lord, stop me if I'm making a terrible mistake by talking about this!*

A warm peace flowed over as she set her cup down, determined to plow ahead. "It's just been since she . . . since she found out she was pregnant."

She paused, watching Jenny's reaction. The older woman raised her thin eyebrows, but Laura saw no shock in her pale blue eyes. Instead she reached across the table and laid her hand on Laura's forearm. "Go on. I'm listening."

Encouraged, Laura took a deep breath and continued, letting the story spill out as she herself had learned of it, finally finishing with what she'd overheard at the Williamses' home earlier that day.

Jenny's eyes widened at that final bit of news. "That must have been very difficult for you to hear."

Laura nodded, hating the tears that threatened, determined to keep them at bay. "It was. I'm still trying to work through it. I wanted so much to confront Megan about it on the way home this afternoon, but I decided to wait."

"A wise decision, I'm sure." She squeezed Laura's arm.

"But he . . . he raped her." Laura shuddered, and she knew Jenny felt it beneath her hand that still lay on Laura's arm. "How do I ever get past that? It was one thing to accept that their relationship crossed the line and my daughter was going to have a baby, even though she didn't have a husband. But . . . but to think she was forced into it, that he—"

"Laura." Jenny's forceful speaking of her name drew her attention. She stopped speaking and listened.

"Didn't you just tell me that you heard Megan say something about accepting part of the guilt herself—for not drawing boundaries soon enough in their relationship?" Jenny shook her head. "That doesn't condone his actions, of course. Nothing does. But it does help explain—just a bit—why it happened and why Megan still has some feelings for the young man."

Laura felt the heat rise to her cheeks. "No. It does not excuse what he did, nor does it even help to explain it. Part of me wants to see Alex Williams behind bars for what he did." She leaned forward. "Jenny, my daughter should not have to have an illegitimate baby because she was raped."

For the first time Laura perceived a flicker of shock pass through her friend's eyes. "Are you suggesting . . . abortion?"

Though the thought had teased at the fringes of Laura's thoughts since she'd first learned of the pregnancy, she'd not allowed herself to say or even think the word. But now, there it was. *Abortion*. A word that represented everything she'd fought against for years. A word she'd told countless others meant the taking of a life—one of the most helpless lives among us, one who'd had nothing to do with the circumstances of its conception.

Laura knew she should say something to explain herself—to defend her thoughts and feelings. But before she could speak, Jenny rose to her feet.

"Wait here. I have something I want to give you."

In moments Jenny was back, carrying a large package, wrapped in Christmas paper and bows. "This is for you." She set in on the table between them. "I just finished wrapping it before you called, but now it's time to open it. Please."

Frowning, Laura steadied her trembling hands and carefully unwrapped the soft package, halfway suspecting what she would find. She was right. The beautiful quilt that had been the basis for their many lunchtime discussions now lay folded on the table in front of her.

"But . . . why are you giving it to me?" Laura tore her gaze from the quilt and looked up at Jenny, who still stood beside the table.

"Because I believe you're the one God intended me to give it to all along." She smiled and sat back down. "I never know who the recipient of my Christmas quilts will be until I'm done. I finished the very last bit of it today and then asked the Lord to show me who it was for. That's when you called. And I must admit, I wasn't surprised, though I had no idea you were about to become a grandmother."

Laura felt her eyes widen. A grandmother? No, she wasn't ready for that—at least not under these circumstances. She shook her head. "I don't believe this quilt is for me, and certainly not because I'm going to be a grandmother. This baby should never have been conceived. How can I accept such an event, let alone rejoice in it?" The tears got the better of her then and spilled out onto her cheeks. "It's just too hard, Jenny. Can't you see that? I can't do it. It's just too hard."

Jenny picked up a corner of the quilt and held it as she spoke. "Elizabeth wasn't the only one who didn't know what she would be when she grew up. None of us knows that until we get there. But if we are to fulfill God's purpose for our life, we need to remember the one thing that our Little Shy did know, even as a child: that whatever she would be, it would be hard. Serving God is seldom easy, my dear. But it is always—always—the right thing to do. And that means making our choices based on His standards, not our own—regardless of the circumstances or consequences."

Their eyes locked as Laura took a tissue from the box on the table and blotted her face. Then, slowly, she nodded and took the quilt from her friend.

Epilogue

SNOW HAD FALLEN THROUGHOUT THE NIGHT, but at least Megan had made it home safe and sound the night before. And today she'd explained to her mom that, since the snow had stopped and the roads were clear, she needed to go see Alex on her own. It was time.

Now they sat in front of the crackling fireplace in the Williamses' family room, with Megan wishing the warmth could melt the awkwardness between them. But she'd finally spoken the words—told Alex about the baby—and now she waited for his reaction. She had expected stronger emotions as she spoke—sweating palms, a racing heartbeat—but all she felt now was relieved.

Alex sat next to her on the couch, his head in his hands. She could only imagine how difficult a time he was having absorbing such life-changing news. She was still working on doing that herself.

At last he lifted his head and ventured a look in her direction. His eyes pleaded with her as he spoke. "What are we going to do?"

She swallowed. "I'm not sure. I plan to finish the semester, and then I may come home and stay with Mom until the baby's born. I'll do what I can to keep up on my studies, but I'm not going to kid myself that it will be easy. Still, I feel I need Mom's support right now, more than

I need to be in school. I can always go back later." She paused. "Or not."

Alex shook his head. "It's not fair—not to you. You're the one who was so serious about med school and becoming a doctor. And now—"

"And now we'll take it a day at a time," she said, interrupting his protest. "All I know for sure at this point is that I'm going to keep the baby. I considered adoption, and maybe, if I were a few years younger or didn't have my mother's support, that might be my best choice. But I . . . I think I can handle it as a single mom." She took a deep breath. "I've thought about it a lot—prayed about, considered my options—and I believe it's the most responsible choice for me to make. Besides, my mom showed me it can be done."

Tears sprang into Alex's brown eyes. "I know I have no right to ask, but . . . can I be involved somehow? I'd really like to be."

Megan's heart squeezed. This was the part of the equation she hadn't been able to work out yet. Her feelings for Alex were still too confusing. "Thank you. And I'm sure you will be. But . . . right now I just don't know what that looks like."

Alex nodded. "Sure. I understand. And that's a fair and honest answer. But somehow I'll take care of my financial responsibility. That's important for the baby."

He was right, though Megan wished she could tell him she didn't need his money, that she could take care of their child by herself. But as he said, his financial help would be important for the baby.

"So that's it." Alex's tone was resigned, though his expression screamed heartbroken.

"Except for one thing." Megan took his hand in hers and looked firmly into his eyes. "I just want you to know that whatever happens, however all this turns out . . . I forgive you. You told me the last time we talked that you've received God's forgiveness, and I wanted to be sure you knew that you had mine too. I just . . . I just hope you'll forgive me for letting our relationship get to the point that you felt justified in doing what you did."

Tears sprang into Alex's eyes, and she could tell he was struggling to speak. "Thank you," he said at last. "As long as I know that, I can deal with all the rest. But Megan, it wasn't your fault—none of it. But yes, absolutely, if you need me to forgive you for whatever part you think you played in this, then I forgive you."

Megan smiled. She had no idea what tomorrow would bring, let alone how things would turn out with the life that grew inside of her. But both she and Alex now knew the One who held the future in His hands, so regardless of what lay ahead, it was time to step into that future with confidence.

THE END

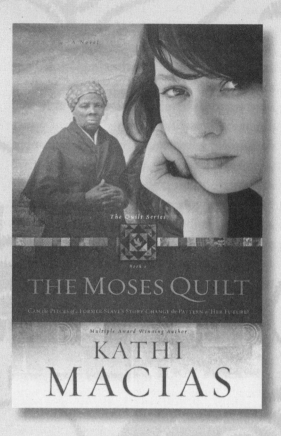

Acknowledgments

We acknowledge the following references and resources in the writing of *The Doctor's Christmas Quilt*:

Nancy Kline, *Elizabeth Blackwell: A Doctor's Triumph* (Berkeley, CA: Conari Press, 1997).

Wikipedia, "Elizabeth Blackwell," http://en.wikipedia.org/wiki/Elizabeth_Blackwell.

Notable Names Database (NNDB), "Elizabeth Blackwell," http://www.nndb.com/people/947/000162461/.

National Library of Medicine, "Biography: Dr. Elizabeth Blackwell," Changing the Face of Medicine, http://www.nlm.nih.gov/changingthefaceof medicine/physicians/biography_35.html.

Steven Ertelt, "Herstory: First US Woman Doctor Elizabeth Blackwell Opposed Abortion," LifeNews.com, http://lifenews.com/2007/03/15/nat-2987/?pr=1.

New Hope® Publishers is a division of WMU®, an
international organization that challenges Christian believers
to understand and be radically involved in God's mission.
For more information about WMU, go to wmu.com.
More information about New Hope books
may be found at NewHopeDigital.com
New Hope books may be purchased at your local bookstore.

Use the QR reader on your
smartphone to visit us online at
NewHopeDigital.com

If you've been blessed by this book,
we would like to hear your story.
The publisher and author welcome your comments and
suggestions at: newhopereader@wmu.org.